Y/N

Y/N

a novel

Esther Yi

ASTRA HOUSE ∧ NEW YORK

Astra House
A Division of Astra Publishing House
astrahouse.com
Printed in the United States of America

Publisher's Cataloging-in-Publication data
Names: Yi, Esther, author.
Title: Y/N : a novel / Esther Yi.
Description: New York, NY: Astra Publishing House, 2023.
Identifiers: LCCN: 2022915583 | ISBN: 9781662601538 (hardcover) | 9781662601545 (ebook)
Subjects: LCSH Popular music—Korea (South)—Fiction. | Fans (Persons)—Fiction. | Korean Americans—Fiction. | Berlin (Germany)—Fiction. | Seoul (Korea)—Fiction. | BISAC FICTION / General
Classification: LCC PS3626 .I4 Y6 2023 | DDC 813.6—dc23

First edition
10 9 8 7 6 5 4 3 2 1

Design by Richard Oriolo
The text is set in Walbaum MT Std.
The titles are set in Walbaum MT Std.

Y/N

1. A Pack of Boys

THE PACK OF BOYS HAD released their first album in Seoul two years ago, and now they were selling out corporate arenas and Olympic stadiums all over the world. I was familiar with the staggering dimensions of their popularity, how the premiere of their latest music video had triggered a power outage across an entire Pacific island. I knew the boys were performers of supernatural charisma whose concerts could leave a fan permanently destabilized, unable to return to the spiritual attenuation of her daily life. I also knew about the boys' exceptional profundity in matters of the heart, how they offered that same fan her only chance of survival in a world they'd exposed for the risible fraud that it was.

At least this was what I'd derived from hours of listening to Vavra. As her flatmate, I was subject to her constant efforts at proselytization. But the more she wanted me to love the boys, the more they repulsed me. The healthy communalism of feeling they inspired, almost certainly a strategy to expand the fandom, desecrated my basic notion of love. I could love only that which made me secretive, combative, severe—a moral disappointment to myself and an obstruction to others. So when Vavra knocked on my door to announce that her friend had fallen ill, freeing up a ticket to the boys' first-ever concert in Berlin, I declined.

"But this concert will change your life," she said. "I just know it."

"I don't want my life to change," I said. "I want my life to stay in one place and be one thing as intensely as possible."

Vavra widened her eyes in affected compassion. In the year since she'd let me, an online stranger, move into her apartment, her tireless overtures of care and my circumventions of them had come to form a texture of cohabitation that could almost be called a friendship. What I feared most wasn't death or global cataclysm but the everyday capitulations that chipped away at the monument of seriousness that was a soul; my spiritual sphincter stayed clenched to keep out the cheap and stupid. Still, Vavra was inadvertently training me in the art of self-delimitation, and for that I couldn't help but feel a bit grateful. I returned my gaze to the book open on the desk before me.

"You look like a scholar," Vavra said. "But you aren't one."

"Thank you," I said, gratified.

"What I mean is, you don't do anything with what you read. What about teaching? You could be shaping young minds."

"How? I can't even shape my own."

"If the boys were to think that way, they wouldn't be where they are now," Vavra said. "They're unafraid to leave a mark on other lives, possessing as they do an unshakable faith in their own genius."

She shut her eyes and disappeared into worship. When she opened them again, she smiled with condescension, as though she'd just been to a place beyond my understanding. But her return to normalcy, to our shared world of stultified passion, struck me as a failure of commitment. I realized then that if I'd yet to follow her to this other place, it was only because I knew I might never come back. It wasn't revulsion I felt but fear that I would befoul myself beyond recognition. Irked by my cowardice and seized, too, by perverse curiosity, I wondered for the first time what it would be like to love the boys.

Two hours later I found myself following Vavra into a crowded arena. Our seats, located toward the rear, offered a meager view of the stage, forcing my attention onto a screen that served as the backdrop. This screen, as large as a Berlin apartment building lying on its side, reproduced the happenings onstage with astonishing clarity, so that when the five boys drifted in as if by accident, heads bowed and hands clasped over their stomachs, I couldn't fathom how their real bodies, as small as grains of rice from where I stood, would survive an evening at the feet of their gigantic images. Thousands of women erupted into shrieks. I remembered Vavra telling me that incidents of shattered eardrums at the boys' concerts were rising, prompting the entertainment company that managed them to recommend earplugs. But I saw none being worn by the fans around me. They were finally breathing the same air as the boys; now was not the time to be less of a body.

The boys stood in a line, their heads still bowed. They appeared freshly reprimanded. Their outfits began with black derby shoes and black trousers, blooming into tops that bespoke their individual personalities. Each boy was named after a celestial body; it went without saying that none of them was named Earth. I didn't know which boy was called what. Vavra was shouting for all five again and again, taking care, on principle, not to say one name more than another.

But I was no egalitarian. I'd already decided that the boy on the far left bothered me most. He wore a pink silk button-down with oversize cuffs that obscured his hands save his fingertips, which gripped the hem with desperation, as if he might fly out of the shirt. His hair was a shade of blond that matched his complexion exactly; skin seemed to be growing out of his head. When he looked up, he revealed an unremarkable face, somehow flat, eyes narrow like the space between two slats of a window blind. But his plainness seemed a calculated strategy to foreground the intensity of his gaze, which discorded with the stony coolness of his pallor. The pose he held should have been impossible: his trunk was perfectly vertical, but his neck jutted forward at an angle so wide that his head, held erect, seemed to belong to another torso entirely. It was the neck that disturbed me. Long and smooth, it implied the snug containment of a fundamental muscle that ran down the body all the way to the groin, where, I imagined, it boldly flipped out as the penis.

The stage lights turned red and shuddered into a new constellation, casting long shadows down the boys' faces. Music began—atonal synths encased in a rib cage of driving percussion—and the boys erupted into dance. They never used backup dancers, according to Vavra, because they considered it a cheap trick to pad themselves out with a horde of comparatively homely boys. So there they were, five lonely specks on a vast black stage. They faced each other in a circle and passed between them an invisible ball of energy. Upon the heady climax of the chorus, they turned around and flung out their arms, palms upturned, as if giving their prismatic harvest over to the surrounding emptiness.

The boys sang:

"What does it mean to die on this planet? Aloneness, despair, confusion. A human being is a particle of dust in a galaxy. And what does it mean to live on this planet? Creation, desire, collision. A human being is a galaxy in a particle of dust."

I remembered Vavra saying that most nights the pack of boys, after the rigorous training of their bodies, washed up and then gathered in their living room to study the classics of art and literature. Like a civilization, the boys entered new eras, one for each album. In preparation for their current era, they'd pored over a Korean translation of Sophocles, troubled by Oedipus's decision to blind himself. Yes, he'd been woefully ignorant of the truth—why not, then, gouge out two new holes on his face, for two more eyes, for double the sight? The album, a statement of protest against Oedipus's capitulation to darkness, celebrated too much seeing, too much light.

My eyes kept returning to the boy with the disturbing neck. The others conveyed depth of feeling by exaggerating their movements or facial expressions; I had no trouble understanding the terms of their engagement with the world. But the boy with the disturbing neck followed an inscrutable logic. I could never predict his next move, yet once it came along, I experienced it as an absolute necessity. He seemed to control even the speed at which he fell from the air, his feet landing with aching tenderness, as if he didn't want to wake up the stage. His movements: fluid, tragic, ancient. Every flick of a joint happened at the last possible moment. He never geared up. He was always already there.

Each boy stood at the head of a triangular formation in turn and sang a bar, prompting the screams in the arena to peak five times. When the boy with the disturbing neck surged forward to take the helm, my eyes filled with tears. Confronted by the tetanic twitching of his individuality under the smooth skin of teamwork, I saw all the more clearly what was different about him, and I knew I loved him because I liked him better than the others.

His voice was a pink ribbon whipping in the wind:

"I used to stand still in one place to observe the world with care. Now I'm running as fast as possible, seeing as fast as possible, yet even this isn't enough, for all I can see at any moment is the street ahead of me before it disappears over the horizon. Will you please flatten out the earth so that I can see ahead of me forever?"

I'd never been able to keep Vavra's exhaustive profile of each boy tethered to a name or a face. But the body onstage extracted details from the depths of my memory, and they spun like thread around the spool of a particular name: Moon. I remembered that Moon, at twenty, was the youngest in the group. He'd been the child prodigy of a ballet company in Seoul, performing every lead role until the age of fourteen, when he was recruited by the entertainment company. Four years later, he'd almost failed to earn a place among the pack of boys because the company president, known as the Music Professor, had been skeptical of Moon's ability to subordinate the idiosyncrasy of his dance to the needs of the group. Details that had been vivid without meaning, applicable to any one of the boys, were now indispensable to the evocation of Moon. It made perfect sense, what Vavra had once told me, how he ate heavy foods right before bed because he liked waking up to find his body slim and taut, proof of the metabolic intensity of his dream life.

I was being sent to the other side; I was having what Vavra had once described as my First Time. But unlike losing my virginity, which I'd anticipated with such buzzing awareness that I'd been more certain I would have sex than die someday, I'd never known to expect Moon. My First Time, experienced at the age of twenty-nine, made me wonder about all the other first times out there to be had. The world suddenly proliferated with secret avenues of devotion.

Several songs later, the boys returned to standing in a line. As Sun, the oldest member at twenty-four, spoke in Korean, translations in English and German trickled across the screen. The boys were halfway through their first world tour, he said, which had begun two months ago in Seoul, after which they'd traveled east to meet their fans in the Americas. Their journey had now taken them to Europe, he said, and they'd decided to surprise their families by flying them out to a continent that they, the boys included, had never visited before.

Each boy faced the camera that fed into the screen to deliver a statement of gratitude to his family. Only Moon, last to speak, walked to the edge of the stage, shielded his eyes from the lights, and peered directly into the crowd.

"Mom, Dad, Older Sister," he said. "I can't see you. I love you. Therefore, where are you?"

His use of "therefore" stunned me.

.   .   .

THE SOUND OF string instruments, melancholic and slow, filled the arena. Moon approached center stage and stood there alone. He was wearing a black blindfold. Everyone in the crowd raised their phones, situating thousands of Moons before me.

He sang that there had been a time when he couldn't bear to cross a room in the presence of others. He didn't want anyone to know the shape of his body, so he wore shirts that hung down to his knees. The fact that he had a face distressed him. If only it could remain hidden like the secret of his groin. But then he met me. Finally, he could bear to be seen. I looked at him so much, more than anyone ever had, that it left him no room to look at himself. That had been the problem, the looking at himself.

"Cock the gun of your eyes," he sang. "I will make myself easy to shoot."

In unison, everyone raised a hand and stretched their thumbs and index fingers apart into pistols aimed at Moon. I couldn't follow along, as my arms were crossed in order to thwart any flare-ups of agency that might disturb my state of perfect passivity, which I needed to maintain so that Moon could act upon me as much as possible.

In the instrumentals, a pistol fired. Thousands of wrists spasmed. Moon, struck in the chest, stumbled backward. I thought he would fall over, but instead he began pivoting on one foot, submitting to the long stream of the crowd's bullets.

His head went first. His arms followed, then his torso, which, dense with organs, forced his other leg into swinging accompaniment. I finally understood that his shirt was the pink of a newborn's tongue. He was tasting the air with his body. It would always be the first day of his life.

He came to a stop and tore off the blindfold. My eyes moved between the screen, where I could see the contours of a bead of sweat dangling from the tip of his nose, and the stage, where his whole body was a tiny blur. I didn't know which I wanted more of, the precise reproduction or the imprecise actuality. He began to walk down a runway that extended from the main stage all the way to the center of the arena floor. On-screen, I saw the bead of sweat wobble, then fall off and disappear from view, likely splattering the floor. Moon tucked in his chin and gazed up at a sharp angle, as if seducing the same person he was threatening to fight. And this person was me. He was walking right in my direction.

I began pushing through the crowd. Angry strangers tried to block my way. I couldn't blame them, I was being a very bad fan. But I felt no solidarity. I excised them from my perception of space. All went quiet in my mind. Moon and I were alone in the arena, headed for each other. I would jump onto the stage and force him to look into my eyes. For a single moment in time, I would be all that he saw. I knew I'd be condemned for imposing on him my individual humanity, divorced from the crowd, but I didn't care, I was a person, I knew this if nothing else, that I was a person, however hapless, however void.

Moon grew from tiny to small, from small to less small. I begged him to become as large as I was to myself, but the closer he came to reaching the size of a normal person, the more I sensed he'd never get there. We stopped moving at the same time: he reached the end of the runway, while I couldn't penetrate the crowd any further. He threw back his head in dreamy surrender, exposing a limestone column of neck almost as long as his face. The cartilage supporting his larynx protruded like a spine. Blue veins ran up the neck and branched off across his mandible. Life swarmed just under his skin. The neck's language was of suppression, unlike that of his face, where the jungle inside his body oozed free through his eyes, nose, and mouth. Vavra's mistake had been to draw rational strokes of narrative, compelling me to understand everything about Moon at once. But all I'd needed was to begin with the singularity of his neck.

A steel cord descended from the ceiling. Moon lowered his head, casting his neck back into shadow, and attached the cord to a buckle on his waist. Every light in the arena was pointed at him. He stood still and endured it. He was a gift forever in the moment of being handed over. But he couldn't be had. Hunger pierced me. I wanted something, and I wanted all of it, but I didn't dare want Moon, because if it was that simple, it was also that impossible.

"I will be you when I grow up," he sang. "You will be me when you are born again."

When the cord lifted him away into the dark firmament of the arena, I didn't say goodbye. I knew I would see him again, that I was doomed to see him always. He had his eyes shut and his arms hanging at his sides, as if surrendering to the controls of a divine force. His hands were curled into loose balls. It made me sick to imagine just how moist his palms must be.

I WORKED FROM home as an English copywriter for an Australian expat's business in canned artichoke hearts. My job required me to credibly infuse the vegetable with the ability to feel romantic love for its consumer. I'd always felt a kind of aristocratic apathy about the task, but in the days following the concert, I avoided my boss's calls altogether, nauseated by the prospect of speaking seriously about such unserious work.

Instead, I spent hours copying a long note that Moon had written by hand for his fans on the occasion of his twentieth birthday. I coveted his handwriting: narrow and angular, flowing across the page with energy and spasming in its higher reaches. I had no Korean handwriting of my own, having grown up speaking the language but almost never writing in it. I cried out in Korean whenever I accidentally touched scalding water, but that slower pain of conducting the relationship I had with myself—this required English. "I like aging before your eyes," Moon had written. "It makes me feel like a story you'll never get sick of." By the fifth time I copied the note, I could compose the text from memory. His hand, even his ideas, had begun to feel like my own.

My phone bleated from my bed for the only reason it was now allowed to bleat: Moon was about to begin a livestream. I entered to find him lying across the crisp white sheets of a hotel bed in Dubai, holding the phone over his face. I lay on my stomach and gazed down at him, phone flat on the mattress. His eyes were heavy with exhaustion. I hoped he would do nothing interesting. His normalcy steeped the two of us in a new intimacy.

"Hello, Liver," he murmured.

The pack of boys called their fans "livers" because we weren't just "expensive handbags" they carried around. We kept them alive, like critical organs. I suspected they used the English word "liver" because it sounded like "lover." They could be coy like that. But I would much rather be Moon's liver than lover.

"I just returned from the buffet downstairs," he said. "There were a hundred different kinds of food to choose from, yet I managed to fill my plate with only the wrong choices. Have you at least eaten well today?"

"Please," I typed in English. "Save your insipid affection for the others. Meals shatter my focus. I can't believe I have to eat three times a day. Where's the ritual that matters?"

Moon's eyes skittered wildly as he tried to read the comments flooding the chat window. Almost as soon as a comment appeared, it flew out of view, overtaken by another, usually in a different language. One fan, a vegan, had looked up the hotel's menu and was now cataloging every animal represented therein so as to love Moon "without illusions." But what I sensed was the fan's desire to be masticated by Moon, just as those animals had been, and to bring him comparable pleasure.

I could hear the bedsheet rustle at the slightest movement of his body, but he couldn't hear the collective din that his fans, numbering in the thousands, were making on bedsheets all over the world. I tried to pretend that no one else was there, that Moon and I were floating alone in virtual space. This exercise fatigued me, especially when I found myself wondering whether I should keep my lips open or shut. The fact of the matter was that he couldn't see me. Even the possibility of looking dumb in front of him was a privilege beyond my reach.

Moon began to laugh deep in his throat. He plushly shut a single eye. He was the only person I knew who could wink sincerely.

He said, "You're up all night worrying about whether I'm getting enough to eat."

He wasn't wrong.

"When my belly is gone, you miss it. But when my belly returns, you miss how my ribs used to protrude. So what is it you really want?"

He was completely justified in asking.

I tapped at my phone with vigor: "I do hope you skip the occasional meal. When you're on the thinner side, your soul becomes more visible, almost hypodermic. You become a pure streak of energy, like the blue flame of a blowtorch. But the entertainment company better not put you on a diet. That would be disgustingly presumptuous. You know best how to flagellate yourself. No company can be as perverse as yo—"

I'd reached the maximum character count. I pressed enter and watched my block of text disappear into a stream of far pithier messages.

"So much English," Moon said. "Let me run some of this through a translator." He fiddled with his phone and squinted. "Based on what I'm seeing, you're either poets or idiots. And here, it's not even a translation. It's just the Korean pronunciation of the English words. The English words must have no correspondents in Korean. My god. What's this inconceivable thing you want to say to me?"

He released a soft groan. Sensing he would log off soon, I begged him to lower the phone so that I would know what it was like to have his face close to mine. He froze, seeming to lock eyes with me. A luxurious docility permeated his expression, and his lips cracked open into a smile that hinted at the black velvet rooms inside of him. Then the whole video blurred.

His left eye filled the frame. It was wide-open, tense; I gathered he was no longer smiling. I had the strange feeling that I wasn't witnessing the transmission of a reality as it unfolded thousands of kilometers away in Dubai but awakening to that which had always been in my bed. This eye had always been lurking among the tired folds of my sheets, rigid with attention to my small life, even to the dark wall of my back at night. I drew closer to the screen. Beyond its quadrilateral parameters lay the rest of Moon's face, his neck, his whole body. We regarded each other without moving or speaking. I knew better than to think that he'd read, much less chosen to obey, my request. But this was of no importance. I didn't need the help of wild fortune to be alone with him.

I wrapped my arms around his neck and held him tight, turning us away from the world and toward each other. The radiator was pumping heat into my room, and the lights were low. The screen resolution was so poor that I couldn't tell where the brown of his iris ended and the black of his pupil began. I was transfixed by this circle of inchoate darkness. But the more I searched it for a flicker of anima, the more it flattened out into sheer color, and abruptly the eye dislocated from Moon, becoming hideous, hieroglyphic.

"Forgive me," he said. "But my arm is so very tired."

His eye shut; the screen darkened. The sheets underneath me suddenly went cold.

"All of me is tired," Moon said. "In my stomach there is camel meat, but in my head there is nothing."

Then he logged off. His voice had cracked while saying "There is nothing." I made an hour-long loop of that phrase alone so that I could study this moment of unbelievable cuteness. "There is nothing," he blared on repeat, making my speaker shake. Vavra pounded angrily at my door. I clenched my fists and bit down on my tongue. But given all that I felt, I needed to do more. I looked around my room and picked up a book from my desk. "There is nothing," Moon said. "There is nothing." I flung the book to the floor. My heart softened at the sight of its forbearance, how it lay butted up against the wall in quiet recovery. So I got on my knees and turned to the first page, promising to read with care. But the words streamed by without making an impact. All I wanted was a single sentence that radiated truth, yet I found myself turning page after page, faster and faster, accruing small cuts all over my hand, as if I were grappling with the mouth of a rabid dog.

2. So Much Human

MASTERSON AND HIS FLATMATES WERE hosting a party in German. I would join a group conversation, picking up the main ideas but knitting them together too late, so that by the time I not only had something to say but also knew how to say it, the conversation had moved onto a new topic entirely. For example, Masterson's friend said, "Everyone is born good at heart. I don't hate my enemies, but the society that has made them that way," after which I said, "I like everything bad that has ever happened to me."

Sick of talking, I sank into an armchair and traced the shapes of everyone's movements around the room. All the attendees were around thirty and finishing up advanced degrees in the humanities or social sciences, with side projects in art or politics. They were teetering between professionalism and the few fruitless ways in which they might deny its inexorable power. They needed their virtuous distractions so as to let their careers fortify as if unsuspectingly—until the balance collapsed, much to their secret relief. Then would come the soft decline of the spirit, which, of course, wasn't without its occasional pleasures.

Everyone was ambulating but Masterson. He was profusely approached. He sat on a window ledge to my right on the far side of the room, cigarette caught between two bony fingers, legs outstretched and hooked at the ankles. He was responding in patient detail to the casual inquiry of a guest, who appeared disquieted by this unmerited show of interest. Everything about Masterson was long, even his thoughts. I was covertly watching him through an oblong mirror on the wall to my left. I hoped everyone would leave soon. What I liked doing most was to lie naked and absolutely still underneath him in bed and to stare into his eyes with no expression on my face. I was happy in those moments because I became nothing, just a scale for his weight.

A woman seated herself on my armrest, obstructing my sensual contemplation.

"What are you doing?" I asked in German. It was easier to be aggressive in a foreign language.

"I'm writing a dissertation," she said. "You must have heard the saying that the pen is mightier than the sword. Well, its usage has vanished from popular literature in recent years.

What has taken its place is the comparison of the pen to a gun. This reflects, I hypothesize, the growing awareness that the act of writing kills quickly and from a great distance. Literature murders—not the reader, as one might expect, but the characters, who are no different from real people. Behind every character is a person out in the world whose sanctity is violated in the process of literary transfiguration. Every black letter on a white page is a bullet."

She must've assumed I'd meant to ask "What do you do?" It disturbed me that anyone could know what it was they did in the abstract.

"Why do you study literature if you hate literature?" I asked in irritation.

"Hate?" The woman turned the word in her mouth as though it were a pebble she'd just found in her food. "Who said anything about hate. No, I don't hate literature." Then she told me I should read the theorist so-and-so. "She'll make sure you never see a book in the same way again."

"How uncalled for," I said.

The woman didn't reply, her gaze having already moved to the other side of the room. She and I would never see eye to eye. So it was with most people.

"How do you know him?" she asked, looking at Masterson.

"I'm his sister," I said.

"Strange," she said uneasily, turning back to me. I could feel her eyes darting around the limited terrain of my face. "He never mentioned having a sister."

"I'm adopted. We haven't seen each other in a while."

"Ah." She sounded only a little less uneasy. "Where are you from? I mean, where are your birth parents from?"

"I don't know."

"You could get a genetic test to find out."

"I am not my cells."

"Then what are you?"

"Well, what are you?"

"My cells are collectively called Lise. They come from Heidelberg."

Only then did I realize who she was. Masterson had told me unforgettable stories about Lise. A year ago, the peaks and troughs of their relationship had reached such amplitudes that within an hour he would go from wanting to marry her to feeling "sick to my stomach" if she so much as uttered his name. Once, while breaking up with her, he'd made the mistake of beginning a sentence with "The way I see it . . ." She'd snatched the glasses off his face and thrown them to the ground, crushing them under her shoe. Whenever Masterson said he didn't love her, she persuaded him otherwise. And then he found that he did love her. If most people looked for someone to love, she, like a tax collector, looked for those who failed to love her and made them pay up.

Lise was describing her favorite buildings in Heidelberg, sweeping her hands through the air to draw precise silhouettes. I imagined her cells slamming against the walls of those buildings—from fighting, but mostly from lovemaking, I hoped—and was amazed she stood in one piece before me.

"Will your cells also die in Heidelberg?" I asked.

"I hope so," she said. "There's a family plot. Where will you die?"

"I don't know," I said.

Lise got up and stood before the oblong mirror. She gazed at Masterson over the shoulder of her reflection, then turned away with tranquil acceptance. My eyes remained on the glass, where Masterson, in the distance, was lowering a beer onto the wooden table beside him. He'd built the table from scratch, enthused by his new plan of us moving in together. I'd once laid a pencil on one end and watched it roll to the other and fall off the edge. Our future dinners would go crashing to the floor; I hoped this meant he wanted to starve me so that there was less of me for others to have. Masterson was now uttering a syllable that required him to bare his teeth, but the back of Lise's head glided into frame and eclipsed his face.

I wanted to concede immediately. I was more convinced by Lise's feelings for Masterson than my own. She knew what she wanted, she'd even had it before, and when she had it again, she would be happy again.

I got up and tried to recover my view of Masterson in the mirror, but now I was impeded by my own reflection, which, to my shock, looked a bit like Moon. I'd never noticed the resemblance before. It was uncanny, the objective similarity of our features. Especially the lips and eyes, their plushness suggesting an overtaxed sensuality, like they'd been doing too much tasting and too much looking. And the black hair, shining like a helmet. But I was the knockoff version in every point of similarity. Moon's beauty wasn't located in a specific physical feature. Instead, there was a tremulous metaphysical orchestration between the various parts of his face. I lacked any such orchestration. If his beauty radiated upon the world, my beauty was local, covering about as much distance as bad breath.

AFTER THE PARTY, I mashed the leftover cake with the palm of my hand. The buttercream squelched tinily in anguish. Masterson, still seated on the window ledge, unhooked his feet, spread his legs apart, and reached for me. I stood between his knees and let him clasp my waist with his hands.

"How are you?" he asked.

I didn't know how to answer in the way he wanted. Personally, whenever I asked, "How are you," I actually meant, "I am not you." I meant, "Your answer should not be like mine." Nothing made me want to end a conversation faster than the words "Oh, that reminds me of the time . . ." I did not want to remind anyone of anything. I did not like to be related to.

In silence, I raised my caked hand to Masterson's mouth. He sucked my fingers one by one, tongue lurching over every knuckle. I was finally starting to enjoy myself. I could tell because I wished I had more body for the world to work upon. Masterson licked clean the back of my hand, where a temporary tattoo of Moon's face gradually revealed itself. I still hadn't told Masterson about Moon. In any case, he didn't notice the tattoo, which was so poorly rendered that one couldn't even tell it was supposed to be a person. But I appreciated everything related to Moon, even unrealized intentions.

"Why did you tell everyone you're my adopted sister?" Masterson asked.

"They kept asking me how I knew you," I said. "What a crazy question. I would need at least two more boring parties to explain how I know you."

"We met online," he said. "Is that so hard to say?"

"How dare you," I said. "To reduce it like that. How dare you."

I laid my hands on either side of his head and tugged gently upward, trying to imagine its weight detached from his neck. His forehead spanned no more than three fingers. I sensed that his best ideas resided just behind this remarkable density of bone. His neck, meanwhile, was thin and bird-like—a precarious support.

"Nils nearly threw up when he saw me fondle you in the kitchen," Masterson said. "I had to explain that you're not my sister but the person I'm currently considering being in love with."

"It's been two months," I said. "If you're still considering the possibility, then you'll never be in love with me."

"But I want to be in love with you."

"I never even had a chance to consider it. I loved you as soon as I saw you. I love you resentfully."

"And I want to love you joyfully. Even considering being in love with you makes me happy. I want that happiness to continue in the actual loving of you. Give me time. I can't wait to love you one day."

In his room, we lay on either side of a blade of moonlight running down the length of his bed. We studied each other. A drunken altercation out on the street began and ended by the time we came together with murmurs of relief. Vivid minutes passed. Then I became extremely thirsty. I looked down. Masterson seemed to have set aside his own pleasure like some discrete object and returned to my body with a noble sense of purpose, embarking on touches that I experienced, to my perturbation, as repayment of some kind. But I demanded nothing from Masterson except that he never hold me back from loving him.

I shut my eyes. The darkness behind my lids gradually took on the coherence of a structure. I was back in the concert arena, but there was no crowd this time. I watched alone from the floor as Moon moved down the runway, the esophageal clicks of his shoes echoing throughout the space. When he reached the end of the stage, he jumped onto the floor and continued in my direction. I stood still, luxuriating in the certainty of being arrived at. Nothing in this colossal emptiness could distract him away from me. When he finally stood before me, I took his hand and led him out of the arena into a darkness void of stars, in the depths of which awaited Masterson's bed.

Moon lay on his back. I crawled on top of him and brushed the hair out of his face. He looked back at me with pure recognition. Both encouraged by his gaze and unable to bear it, I closed my eyes and kissed him. But it was like pressing my lips against the back of my own hand. I felt what he felt of me; I felt what I felt like. With a start, I realized I had no sexual desire for Moon. My sexuality simply loved his sexuality, totally and unblinkingly, without my needing to know anything about what he did with his. I felt disgraced—by life, its strange personal commandments—that I couldn't simply want him.

Sensing my hesitation, Masterson roughly pushed me aside and straddled the boy. The moon cast a milky net upon the surface of the bed, illuminating the entire length of the latter's body, while Masterson's torso jutted upward into the surrounding darkness. He unbuttoned the boy's shirt down the line. Two panels of pink silk slid away from each other, revealing an expanding bar of luminescent skin. Masterson tugged off the boy's pants, then his underwear.

"How are you?" Masterson asked.

Moon, gazing up at his lover with sorrowful reverence, opened and shut his mouth without making a sound. He had no words for so much human. In frustration, he grabbed Masterson's much larger hands and placed them around his own throat. He angled back his chin, extending his neck as long as possible, then used his hands to signal that Masterson should squeeze hard. Surely he had something to say deep inside, extrudable like toothpaste.

"But how are you?" Masterson asked.

Even tighter, Moon signaled.

Masterson clamped his knees shut against Moon's thighs, throwing his testicles into agitation. Their wizened tenderness audibly skimmed the boy. Masterson began to lower himself onto his young lover, joining that capsule of moonlight, maintaining a grip on Moon's neck all the while. His face was last to emerge from the darkness, drawing close over Moon's and creating, between those two planes, a stratum of shadow. Their lips brushed furtively, never quite kissing. Masterson's exhales were deep and threatening. His martial focus aroused Moon, who, short of breath, opened his mouth and widened the aperture of his throat, enjoying the futile resistance of his neck against the pressure of his lover's hands.

I knew how all of this felt, better than if I had felt it myself. The boy was my ambassador, sent to a foreign land with which my own land was in delicate relations. I'd never visited this country myself, maimed king as I was.

THE NEXT MORNING I awoke to find Masterson lying on his side, reading a book I'd lent him. He glanced over at me, then held out what looked like a playing card.

"Want this back?" he asked. "I found it tucked between the pages."

It was a glossy picture of Moon smiling so hard that his eyes were nearly shut. It had come inside the sleek plastic box containing a thirty-day skincare regimen endorsed by the pack of boys. I'd purchased the elaborate set of hydrating face masks just so I could own this image of Moon's unadulterated joy. But to encounter the picture now, when I least expected it, so unsettled me that I drew back without taking it from Masterson.

"This is Moon, right?" he said.

I rose to a kneel on the mattress in a daze.

"How do you know who Moon is?" I asked.

"Why shouldn't I? I live in the world. I stay abreast. What, are you a fan?"

"No," I said. "I'm not a fan."

I wanted to follow up with what I actually was, but no word came to mind.

"It's a fascinating phenomenon, isn't it?" Masterson said, contemplating the picture.

"What do you mean by 'it'?" I asked suspiciously.

"We once turned to philosophy for an interpretation of God, for that which lies beyond our comprehension. But philosophy has relinquished its authority to data. Now we know too much, especially what people want and how to give it to them. Religion is no longer a site of our interminable struggle with negativity. Religion, shorn of philosophy, is now a vending machine for manifestation and fulfillment. That's why there are so many lowercase gods in this secular, cynical era. Oblivious to the contradiction, we yearn for spiritual practices that will make us worthy of receiving permanent answers and solutions. A boy band like this"—Masterson waved the picture of Moon—"is one such god. Here we have data disguised as philosophy, information disguised as art. We no longer go to church once a week; we attend a stadium concert once a year."

He flashed a broad smile, excited by ideation. I didn't even disagree with him. Still, I had my side of things, which wasn't a side so much as it was its own ecosystem of experience.

"I think I'll use them for my research," he said, peering down at Moon with friendly curiosity. "I'll have to learn everything I can about them."

I snatched the picture out of his hand.

"What?" he said.

"Moon can't be researched," I said. "He's too variable, too alive. We're talking tonight, actually. He'll ask about my day and its key moments of deadlock. He'll ask insightful follow-up questions. He'll say nothing when total seriousness of spirit is called for. But he'll also make me laugh in that spastic, uncontrollable way I never do with you. Like my navel is the twisted end of a sausage coming undone."

Masterson's face had gone murky with confusion, but I could see that the premise of my vitriol was starting to dawn on him.

"You're talking about him as if you know him," he said carefully.

"I do know him. The person I don't know is you."

"Am I supposed to take this seriously?"

"I'm never not serious. I have no idea who you are."

"But you know Moon. How conveniently hard to prove."

I had the spontaneous fantasy of burying my heart inside Masterson's chest, right next to his. But if I couldn't fully integrate myself into his body, then I would exile myself to Irkutsk. Either way, no longer would I have to wrangle with the ambiguity of the distance between us—one day lush proximity, another day chilling estrangement. I tried to think of the meanest possible thing to say:

"He feeds my imagination more than you do."

"Of course he does," Masterson said. "Because he exists in your imagination."

"He's a person breathing, eating, and dreaming in Seoul."

"And I'm a person breathing, eating, and dreaming in Berlin." Masterson reached over to give my thigh a painful squeeze. "And I know you exist."

"You might know I exist, but he knows, unlike you, the most important thing there is to know about me, which is my need for spiritual companionship."

"I think what you mean is that he designs his lyrical content and sexual appeal with the specific intent of exploiting the most basic of human emotions, like loneliness, or the desire for unconditional love, and then derives massive profit from his vampirism."

I rolled off the bed and began to dress, tucking the picture into a pocket.

"He works a hundred times harder at our relationship than you do," I said, jamming my foot into a shoe with an aggressive twist of the ankle. "He has physical therapy every day because his tendons are on the constant brink of snapping. Can you say the same about your tendons?"

WHEN I ENTERED the livestream, I found Moon sitting at a table. Behind him, I recognized the luxury apartment he shared with the other boys in an undisclosed region of Seoul. His eyes were puffy, indicating his fresh departure from the world of dreams. It was morning there. He hummed a wistful tune, his eyes never leaving mine. My teeth felt cold; I was smiling hugely.

"Liver," he murmured. "I would like to get on a train and head straight for you."

I missed him so much that my eyes filled with tears. How was it that I missed someone I'd never met before? Someone I hoped to meet one day. Could this mean it was possible to miss the future?

Moon reached over and moved his phone to reveal Mercury sitting across the table. I was stung by the betrayal, his lack of appreciation for our rare chance to be alone together. So uncomfortable was it to have a negative feeling about Moon that I transposed it onto Mercury, and this wrenching of my emotive focus from one boy to the other gave me vertigo. All I could feel for a few seconds was hatred so intense that I worried my heart might never find its way back to its principal feeling of love for Moon.

"Don't be angry with me," Moon said into the camera. "It's not what you think. I do want to be alone with you. But sometimes I can't stand hearing my own voice for an entire hour."

Mercury was sitting very still and staring down at the table, as if devoting all his rational faculties to grasping the single most depressing idea in the world. He was known as the least talkative among the boys, but still, his mood today struck me as unusually subdued.

"I wish I could hear your voices one at a time," Moon continued. "But if I were to have a conversation with each of you for just one minute, it would take two centuries. So I want to try something out. Pretend Mercury is you. Yes, pretend we're alone in this room together. Type in the chat what you would like to say or do, and Mercury will serve as your representative."

Moon had barely finished speaking when commands began to pour into the chat. Accordingly, Mercury sprang out of his chair and rushed over to a window, where he hid behind the floor-length curtain and peeked out at Moon.

"Don't look at me!" Mercury said. "I'm not ready!"

"For what?" Moon asked.

"To be alone with you."

"There's not much to it. Trust me. I do it all the time."

Mercury unrolled himself from the curtain and cautiously approached the table. He returned to his seat, whereupon a myriad of expressions flashed across his face, from harrowing fear to avuncular satisfaction. He ultimately settled on opening his mouth in awe at such a close-up view of Moon.

"Is there any part of you that's not beautiful?" Mercury asked.

"Show me. Then I'll know for sure that you're a real person."

Moon slid his hands across the table: "My cuticles."

Mercury bent his head over Moon's hands and pushed back one cuticle after another. He tore out excess bits of skin and made a little pile. Then he sprinkled the bits into his mouth and chewed, the working of his jaws suggesting a consistency like that of jerky.

"I love even your dead skin," he said mournfully. "I'm doomed."

Mercury broke into a smile that prefaced inappropriate laughter. But he didn't laugh. Instead, he murmured that he was cold and alone in a convalescent home, then something about wanting to hide under the table whenever a person more beautiful than him entered the room. He smiled the whole time he spoke.

Then he got up and briefly disappeared out of frame. He returned with a candle and lit it with a match.

"Are you burnable?" he asked, grabbing Moon's hand and placing it over the flame. "It's hard to imagine you being made of the same material as me."

"Yes," Moon said. "That really hurts."

"I'll be so mad if you die before me."

"Stop, stop."

Moon had been watching Mercury with tender curiosity, but now he snapped his hand free and glowered at the other boy.

"Is this really how you want to spend the little time we have together?" Moon asked. "Isn't there anything you would like to talk about?"

At this, Mercury came alive with the desire for conversation, but in such excess that a conversation became all but impossible. He broached a vast array of topics:

"Is it true that women in Korea have auras white as snow? How do you like your eggs? May I bear your children? How do I make him agree to be loved by me? Should I say yes? Are you ever embarrassed for me? Don't spare my feelings. Do I look hideous when I scream for you? When I listen to the news, I get jealous of the most horrible event of the day, like a high schooler gunning down his classmates or families getting burned to a crisp by a military strike. I wish I were a horrible event so that you'd hear about me. Hey, why don't you like Dostoevsky?"

Before Moon could reply, Mercury got up from his seat and positioned himself behind Moon. He wrapped his arms around Moon's neck. First, the embrace was friendly. But then a hand wandered across Moon's chest. This hand freed the top button of Moon's shirt. Moon slapped it away. The hand, immediately cowed, retreated to Moon's shoulder and patted it like a business partner. But then the voluptuous spirit that had lived in the hand entered Mercury's lips, and they dropped little kisses along the area where Moon's shoulder curved into neck. Mercury's lips eventually reached the Adam's apple, which was bobbing with anxiety.

"Please . . ." Moon said.

Mercury's hands leapt to his face. He staggered away in reverse, then dropped out of view, somewhere below the table.

"Am I making you uncomfortable?" I could hear him saying. "Will this go down in your psychological history as the moment it all changed for the worse? Will you have to recover from me? I'm ashamed of how bad I am at living. To become a human being is the only task, and I'm dimly aware that its accomplishment requires that I run the hands of truth, briefly gifted from above, over the most secret part of another person. But no one will let me. So should I kill myself? Tell me how. I want to pull it off with such dark elegance that it makes you proud."

"No no no," Moon said.

He slid out of the chair and lowered himself to the floor, also disappearing from view. Only weeping could be heard. Because its source was nowhere to be seen, the weeping seemed to live on my side of the screen, and I felt that if I were to shut my laptop, the weeping would continue.

I looked at the chat window for the first time since Mercury had begun his work as our medium. Infighting had erupted. The fans who worshipped Moon within the context of a religious practice were outraged by the sacrilege of the fans who wanted a chance at romantic love with him. Both groups, in turn, were exasperated by the wholesome few who just wanted to "get to know him better."

A hand appeared from the side of the frame and veered toward the screen. I turned my face to offer up a cheek, burning in anticipation of the caress I desired from Moon. But as soon as his palm was large enough that I could see its crooked life line, my screen went black and the weeping vanished.

3. fleurfloor

ONE AFTERNOON, SITTING ON THE edge of his bed, head in his hands, Masterson said that, try as he might, he couldn't bring himself to fall in love with me and probably never would.

"Of course not," I said, rolling off the mattress and proceeding to collect my books from his desk. The movements came naturally; getting out of someone's way was my default. "One time I left my journal here as if by accident, hoping you'd sneak a look. But you didn't. How could you possibly love me when you're not in the least curious about me?"

"You're hurt," Masterson said. "You're drawing irrational connections."

"Connections aren't irrational enough. People should jump to more conclusions." I was struck by the impossibility of conveying what I felt, which was crushing disappointment. It was a feeling that a child would have no trouble expressing. "I really am your adopted sister. You know you're supposed to love me, but you don't know how to make the feelings seem organic, like they were always there."

"You may be right," Masterson said with delicacy. "But I know what love feels like. I've felt it before."

"And what does it feel like? Butterflies in your stomach? Makes the hair stand up on the back of your neck?"

"Yes," he said. "You think it's stupid, but yes."

"I don't think it's stupid," I said coldly. "I don't think it's stupid at all."

"You always do this, you bully the feelings right out of everything. I want to feel like I'm coming back somewhere. I want to feel at home with you."

I nodded without meeting his eyes, finding it impossible to argue. He was right in exactly the wrong way. I hugged the books to my chest until I could feel my heart knocking against their covers. Masterson had borrowed and read all of them. Sometimes I imagined us meeting in the room of our mutual reading and continuing—fulfilling—our lives there. But I had no idea how to access this room, and talking about the books only made things worse.

"I want to feel at home with you," he repeated.

Cradling the books, I buried my face in his lap and said he was the stupidest person I'd ever met, even stupider than me.

. . .

I WROTE MASTERSON a letter by hand without thinking. When I was done, I was surprised to see what I'd written: "So many people look at me with their eyes but don't actually see me. You're different. You don't even know I exist, but you see me." There were also lines like "I love you so so so much" and "You are the most rewatchable person I know. Something about you is always new." Realizing what I'd done, I crossed out "asters" in "Dear Masterson" and scratched in a big "o" overhead.

I sealed the letter and mailed it to Masterson.

It was likely he'd have no idea what I was getting at, but better that he have none of the idea than have him grasp most but not all of it. I was tired of making arguments and revelations, of words falling out of my mouth and exploding in another person's face. Such crudeness necessarily introduced error. What I wanted was to speak of intensity without speaking intensely. My dream was of a communicative maneuver so subtle that Masterson's thinking eventually accommodated mine without him realizing it.

There was no reply. So I started writing Masterson another letter addressed to Moon. But I ended up writing a story instead.

It begins with the narrator waiting at a bus stop in Berlin. She rubs her eyes. The accumulation of floaters is spoiling her sight of the world, which is simply there, neither obscure nor clear. But should the world be obscure, she wants a clear view of this obscurity. She turns her head and notices a man sucking on a cigarette with unusual patience. She finds him beautiful and hopes no one else at the bus stop thinks the same. Her perception of beauty shudders at the idea of their agreement.

She approaches the man and asks for a drag. He hands over the cigarette without a word. She sucks on it with such force that the smoke surges into the cavern of her head. She is not a smoker. There is no habit for her to occupy with poise, there is only the raw gesture of desire. She hopes all of this comes across. Eyes watering, she hands back the cigarette.

"I already know I would endure unjustifiable pain for you," she says, slipping a hand into his coat pocket and rubbing the loose change between her fingers.

"Then let's do something together," the man says. "Should we eat? I know I should. But I have no appetite to speak of. I was born with a stomach smaller than my heart, but, look, this entire body of mine"—he gestures down at himself—"is incredibly long. There is so much of me to fuel."

The bus arrives, but the two do not get on. As they walk down the street, the narrator senses they were rudely cut off in a previous life. It is possible, she realizes for the first time ever, to open her mouth and say exactly what she's thinking.

At a cheap bistro, the two share a large flatbread folded around a charred strip of meat. The man eats in a highly forgettable way. She likes this, how the sight of the food nearing his mouth promptly deletes itself. She learns that he is a philosopher named Moon. He learns that she is not much of anything; she describes herself as empty spaces gathered into the shape of a human body. Just before parting ways, they exchange their cell phones so that all they must do in order to reach each other is dial their own number from memory. Their phones have become walkie-talkies for the two of them alone. It's obvious they won't be contacting anyone else ever again.

The next day, the narrator reads Moon's latest book in one sitting and understands everything without knowing what it is that she is understanding. The experience fills her with violent light. She wants to hand her mind a butcher's knife with which to hack away every weak and convenient thought. She also wants to risk the greatest possible confusion. She quickly realizes that these desires are one and the same. The lucid strangeness of the philosopher's work occasionally brings her to tears.

"Thank you for not trying to relate to me," she says, shaking the book like a box of cereal.

Moon writes and publishes another book in a matter of weeks just so that she will have more to read. He leaves his wife and children. So much does she admire his cold decisiveness that she looks forward to suffering the same abandonment in the future. In preparation, she practices holding her breath underwater until all of her is pain.

"Be out in the world with me," she tells him over the phone. "Let's pretend we're video-game characters with multiple chances at life and move into unusual circumstances without fear."

But they do not walk side by side. On the street, she stays several meters behind him so that she is always longing for him. Despite their open mutual understanding that they are in love, they are slow about coming together. They meet seventeen times before they properly touch.

"So this is life," she thinks in the midst of it. "I'm dying."

The philosopher neither dances nor sings. In fact, whenever music plays, he falls utterly still and shuts his eyes. So what makes the philosopher Moon? What makes him Moonish?

It's the neck. Moon the character and Moon the real person are endowed with the same neck. To the narrator's fascination, the longer she looks at Moon's neck, the less human it appears. It's a Rubin vase: she can never see the whole thing at once. It evades her—but with shocking force of personality. The neck explains everything—and how it does so is expressed not by "because" but by "in spite of." Its proximity to the charming undulations of the face brings into sharp relief its possession of an obscenely impersonal will, a fluency in violence, the personality of a shy psychopath.

I sent the scenes to Masterson. Still no reply.

I discovered Archimage not long afterward. The website contained thousands of fan-written stories organized by the celebrity or fictional character featured in them. There were smaller categorizations based on the story's emotive instigation, tagged with what each story "makes you . . ." My favorite stories about Moon almost always had the tag "makes you end friendships." Frankly, most of the stories were unreadable. After all, the authors weren't writers, but fans who had turned to language as a last resort. I could feel the frustration mounting as the prose grew ever more sodden, as the author submitted to yet another cliché, hoping their strange feelings would foment, coherently limbed, out of the primordial soup of failing story. But I preferred these stories to most contemporary novels, which mirrored the pieties of the day with absurd ardor. For all the lone superiority suggested by their tone of moral indignation, these books were mind-numbingly easy to agree with. I preferred reading fans and dead people because they were hard to agree with.

I couldn't stop thinking about my two lovesick characters. So I took my scenes and copied them into a dedicated notebook, then continued the story there. Once I'd completed what felt like a chapter, I typed out the text and published it on Archimage under the username fleurfloor.

Then I dyed my hair completely white. My visual goal was a widow interested in remarrying.

THE PACK OF boys' latest music video reached some incredible number of views, setting yet another world record. The next day, the Berlin chapter of the fandom hosted a celebration in a café. When I arrived, I balked at the threshold, sensing the presence of others like me. There was, slicing a pornographic line through the bloated cheer, a hostile energy that could be produced only by abnormal love for Moon. I wasn't sure how to navigate a space filled with strangers who knew I loved what they loved. It was like going to the sauna, except our naked bodies were identical, which made the embarrassment recursive and pointless.

A young woman approached me:

"Hi, I'm two in Liver age. The day I became a Liver, a pair of large men entered my apartment and offered faster internet service. You?"

"Hi," I said. "I'm an infant. The day I became a Liver, the guy sitting next to me on the subway was reading a book called 'How to Become a CEO.' That's how I knew he wasn't a CEO. I found it horrible to know at a single glance what a person wasn't."

Fans remembered details from their lives in arbitrary connection with the pack of boys. It was how we kept track of time.

The woman, who was the president of the Berlin chapter, asked if I would like to "contribute to the happiness of everyone here." My honest answer was no, but out of politeness, I let her take me behind a folding screen, where four women were getting dressed in thrifted versions of outfits the boys had worn in their record-breaking video. The president pushed a bundle of clothing into my arms.

"You'll make a great Moon," she said.

Once outfitted, the five of us emerged from behind the screen as the hit song played over the speakers. We were greeted by screams of delight. A crew from a local news station followed us around as if we were anthropological subjects. I floated through the room in a pink cape made of imitation silk. Everyone took pictures with me. Some requested I hold their phone so that the picture would capture my extended arm as proof of my personal investment in achieving the image.

"I love you," everyone said.

"I love you more," I said, meaning it. I had to if I wanted to believe that Moon would say the same to me.

Afterward, we split into small groups for "confession sessions." I was startled to see Lise across the table from me, my emulation of Moon's signature sprawled across her forearm in black marker. In the frenzy of an hour ago, I must have given her an autograph without recognizing her. I tried to make eye contact, but she blushed deeply and averted her gaze.

An engineer who specialized in making robotic wrists "swivel in a human way" took full control of the conversation. We were incredibly lucky, he said, to be alive at the same time as the boys during this epochal moment in history. Christianity and capitalism—might he and other fans come together to form a movement to rival even these? Could we take over every other movement and thereby supersede our own particularity to become equivalent to humanity itself? He confessed that his deepest desire was to serve as the prime minister of a nation composed solely of fans and to declare all kinds of edicts.

Lise was next. In a voice trembling with shy excitement, she confessed that she'd come to love Moon without knowing anything about him. It had all started when she'd stumbled upon a piece of Y/N fic, which, she explained, was a type of fanfiction where the protagonist was called Y/N, or "your name." Wherever Y/N appeared in the text, the reader could plug in their own name, thereby sharing events with the celebrity they had no chance of meeting in real life.

Reading her first Y/N story, Lise had learned incredible things about herself: At nineteen, she gave birth to Moon out of wedlock and was forced by her aristocratic family to leave him at an orphanage. He grew up to become a truck driver who specialized in transporting prize horses. This was how she reunited with her son, who strode up to the gates of her estate with a chestnut mare rearing at his side. The two recognized each other without exchanging a word. What commenced was a dreamlike summer in which the pair covered great distances side by side, she on horseback, Moon in his truck . . .

Only after finishing the story did Lise find out about the pack of boys, their fame, how Moon sang and danced alongside the others. But all of this mattered little to her. Hungry to uncover new facets of herself, she began to read one Y/N story after another.

The engineer straightened out his back like a displeased patriarch.

"Y/N fic puts me to sleep," he said. "In order to accommodate the biography of every reader that might chance upon the story, the writer creates a character void of personality. But there can be no story without a proper protagonist. So there is never a story when it comes to Y/N. There are only absurd and arbitrary leaps in plot. All of this amounts to a warning, one I urge you to heed. Anyone who pursues the delusional fantasy of being Moon's chosen one can expect to have their identity wiped out. This"—he gestured at our table, the event—"is so much bigger than you. You are not Y/N. All of us are, all at once."

"No," Lise said without blinking. "Only I'm Y/N. There's been just one time that I wasn't Y/N."

She recounted how, wanting to know what it was like to be neighbors with Moon, she'd started reading a story in which he lived in Berlin. To her disturbance, he turned out to be just like her ex. They were both philosophers, and they read the same books, hung out at the same bars. They even had the same birthmark on the inside of their left thighs, and they both waved like a madman whenever they saw her approaching from a distance.

"The Y/N of that story couldn't have been me," she said, "because that Y/N was too me. The point is that I'm no longer me. I'm Y/N. I've taken my destiny into my own hands, and I've decided that I am now a person who knows Moon."

It appeared that Lise had read my story on Archimage. I tried to meet her eyes once more, but she kept her gaze on the engineer, which I found admirably resilient, given his look of intensifying disdain.

"One person can't possibly be so many different people," he said. "You say you're Y/N, but you're really no one at all. You're the placeholder itself. A vacancy waiting to be filled."

"Exactly," Lise said with a dreamy smile. "Moon is a feat of singularity. There has never been anyone like him and there never will be. He is too specific, too unusual. I must try my hand at being everyone if I am to coincide with him. He stays in one place; I roam endlessly."

I broke in: "But what about your work, your friends, the life you wake up to every morning? Even now—how do you stay real to yourself as you sit here?"

Lips aquiver, she mustered all her strength not to look at me. Irked by her evasion, I pushed on:

"Lise, right? Or do you no longer go by Lise?"

Her eyes jerked in my direction. Her hands flew up to her face.

"I know you're not him," she said in tears. "But I feel horribly excited and embarrassed talking about Moon in front of you. You were only pretending to be Moon, but I already know I would do anything for you. You make me laugh, cry, and scream. You do it all so much better and faster than my ex. You're an advanced machine that's put him out of work. I used to think I could never love anyone else. But when we got back together recently, it lasted just a day. I kept wishing you were our son. I forced him to take pictures with an empty space between us because that was supposed to be you there."

MY BEDROOM HAD a large square window that hinged open like a door. It was Sunday morning. Down below, the unpeopled, unvegetated street gave the impression of having been purged by relentless human activity. The air was dense with the smell of meat cooked in oil, freshly brewed coffee, and cigarettes—all manners of burning substances into deeper tastes. Two young bleary-eyed people dressed in black stumbled in from the left. The most conspicuous thing about them was that they weren't rabid with desire for each other. Church bells rang in the distance. I couldn't imagine anyone sitting in the pews.

I opened my notebook and continued my story about Y/N and Moon:

The couple moves to Seoul so that Moon, an adoptee, can find his birth mother. Neither of them know Korean, so Y/N proposes they take a language course together:

"Me, Korean American. You, Korean German. When we speak in English, you struggle to express yourself. When we speak in German, I struggle to express myself. But if we were to speak in Korean, we'd be at an equal loss."

They sign up, they sit down, they look up at the whiteboard. At home they are up to their knees in workbooks. The phonics, unfamiliar to these two foreigners, add wrinkles around their mouths. Their lips obtain new vectors. They become better at kissing.

Moon learns that his birth mother had been an accomplished dancer who died in a car accident on her way to a performance. He imagines her body, the source of his life, crumpling between the soft seat and the metal wall of the car, every golden drop of dance squeezed out of it. He begins taking dance lessons. But he quickly outgrows teacher after teacher. So he decides to take all of it, art, upon himself. Y/N pushes their furniture aside so that he has more room to practice. She sits in a corner and admires the rapidly expanding vocabulary of his body. They are both shocked by whom he could have been all along. He even composes strange and innovative shapes in bed. She tries to fit her own stiff body into them. Then they breathe and breathe and breathe.

"I envy you," she murmurs, head on his chest. "Now that you know how to dance, you will move through the world differently. You see no roads. You see only kilometers of stage. So fatherless, so motherless. I love you, I love you."

The next day, while practicing, Moon throws his arms into the air. He arches back his head to gaze at his fingers, which straighten out in the manner of an ideal gift-receiver: neither greedy nor making a pretense of apathy. What happens next is a feat of dance that defies description. Y/N, who is hungry to find out everything about her life, senses that the entire range of her possible knowledge lives in this dance move. The impact is oblique and vast, instead of pinched and certain; it seems to her that brushes with the truth have this quality of swathed intensity. The move does not express an emotion of measurable quantity; it is the measure itself. It is too much and nothing at the same time. Moon has oversaturated himself, yet the final balance is zero. His move is what a cup contains but not the cup itself; his move has no container by means of which excess can be conceptualized.

Whatever this move was, I was certain Moon had never struck it before. Yet I was also certain that he was the only person in the world who could.

It was dark outside by the time I published this latest chapter on Archimage. When I got up and stretched my arms overhead, I wondered if I could improvise my way toward the mysterious dance born of my fiction—the move of my Moon dreams. I gave it a try. My entire body exploded in pain. Limbs had to go where they couldn't. Muscles were asked to tense and relax at the same time. My head behaved like its own person—one, I suspected, just released from the penitentiary. It was so hostile, so independent. Out of breath, I collapsed onto the mattress.

That night I had a dream in which my view was overwhelmed by a canine tooth jutting out of Moon's mouth, so large and hooked that he couldn't shut his lips over it. Otherwise, he looked the same. In the world of my dream, everyone knew about this tooth but chose to ignore it. It was so much better for our spirits to see him as beautiful.

4. Infinite in the Negative

THE ANALYTICS DEPARTMENT OF ARCHIMAGE compiled
an exhaustive list of the celebrities and fictional characters featured in its stories. These four-hundred-some individuals were
then ranked according to the number of times they appeared
as the primary subject of a work. I was shocked to find Moon
in first place.

Ever since the concert, I'd learned to accept Moon exactly
as he presented himself, not because I was afraid to discover
some cunning boardroom scheme at the bottom of it all, but
because I was sure that knowing everything would reveal nothing of importance. I didn't need the behind-the-scenes footage
of his performances; I didn't want to go behind anything. My
aim, in fact, was to sink ever deeper into the marshes of fantasy.

All I required was the freedom to dream about Moon. But his first-place ranking made the disturbing suggestion that my imagination, one of the few remaining places where I felt truly free, was actually the site of my dreariest conformity. I knew my feelings for Moon were neither unique nor all that extreme, and I even viewed mass popularity as his rightful due. But writing stories about him was supposed to have represented a higher level of devotion, an elitist kink in the plain template of fandom.

For the first time, I doubted the singularity of my love and thereby its truth. I glimpsed a future where I felt nothing for Moon, as one did, with both relief and melancholy, on the cusp of a breakup. I nearly fainted from disorientation. My love, which I'd considered, not without pride, a destabilizing force, was turning out to be exactly that which stabilized me.

I stared at the list, paralyzed.

All of a sudden, Moon's inclusion struck me as preposterous. It was as if "suffering" or "the divine" had been mixed into a list of character names. Moon was not a character. He was a theme, a universal constant. He was greater than himself. Stretching out from all sides was the terrain of Moon, and I would pitch my tent where no one else thought to. My Moon had nothing to do with the other writers' Moon. My Moon wasn't the Moon of first place. It wasn't first enough, first place. My Moon was the whole list.

.   .   .

DUSK WAS BRUISING the sky. I turned onto a residential street where people who could no longer be called young were disappearing one by one into buildings. These individuals affected an air of frigid beauty, as if to counteract the mortal admission of the vegetables and toilet paper bulging through their canvas bags. As soon as a door shut behind them, a golden shaft of light plunged through the stairwell, making their slow ascents visible even from a distance. In an apartment somewhere, a child repeatedly cried out in disbelief. I envied his indefatigable sensitivity, how he took no account of the increasing familiarity of whatever force was working upon him.

It was the first warm day of the year. The boys were now back in Seoul, concluding their world tour with a performance in the same stadium where they'd inaugurated their journey four months ago. I should've been home, watching a livestream of their final show. Instead, I was walking all over Berlin, moving in ever-enlarging circles and then narrowing in on Masterson's block in order to give him as great a chance as possible of finding me. I knew I could've just called him and demanded a meeting. But I had no desire to foist my presence onto him and preferred to make my body shamelessly available for the obelisk intrusion of his.

It was dark by the time I reached his street. Upbeat trance music was playing in the bar on the ground floor. Outside, the drinks menu was lit up in a glass case like an important poem. I hid under the broken lamp opposite his building. To my relief, his bedroom on the second floor was dark.

Just as I was about to continue on my way, the lights turned on. Masterson appeared at the window. Why, I thought with irritation, was he in the one place in the world where I couldn't be? He looked down at me with a forlorn expression and raised a feeble hand to the glass. Was he trapped in the room against his will? I signaled that I would save him—how I did this was by bursting my hands apart from each other to indicate freedom and release. But then I worried he might interpret this as what I desired between the two of us, so I shyly displayed my palms, then pressed them to my chest. "Your hand—I feel it against my heart," I was saying.

He couldn't tear his eyes away from me. He seemed gripped by melancholic fascination. I knew I had to keep him thinking about me at all costs, for love was the act of thinking about a person in an unusual color; how we perceived the character of that color was always shifting, one moment as disgust, another moment as desire. I had to risk the former to strike the latter.

Masterson gave a small wave. But nothing on his face suggested he was happy to see me. I was still trying to interpret his expression when he looked over his shoulder. He moved his lips, then shook his head with a wry smile. Was there someone in the room with him? He stepped away from the window, leaving a perfect view of a portion of white ceiling where two strips of crown molding came together at a right angle. The mere sight of this corner, with its suggestion of a profound interiority, filled me with pain.

Suddenly, a loud slam. All I could see was Masterson's hand twisting at the wrist to ensure the pressurized lock of the window's side handle. I blinked hard, struggling to understand what had just happened. A white curtain fluttered into place, and the lights shut off. I staggered away in disbelief. The window had been wide open all along. He'd been there, right there. I could've spoken to him, I could've reached in a hand. That was all it would've taken to be with him again—to have run across the street and rolled onto my toes, arm reaching up, hand slipping in.

MOON AND Y/N have been living in Seoul for half a year now. They obtained heritage visas to be able to stay in the country. Y/N has begun working as an English tutor to the morose son of a wealthy businessman.

On her way home from work one evening, Y/N gets off the subway a stop earlier to take a walk. She sees a young man dancing on the concrete plaza by the entrance to a park. She squints through the darkness for a better look—it's Moon. A small crowd, mostly women, to her intense jealousy, has gathered around him. She stands in the back. Why hasn't he told her about these evening exhibitions? What other secrets might he be keeping?

Moon, absorbed in his own languid movements, does not see her. He strikes his elbows against each other, bones audibly clicking, then flares them apart to reveal two fresh bruises shaped like buttons.

Y/N walks home, besieged by sadness.

She lies in bed and deletes every picture of Moon on her phone. She is sick of looking at these pictures on her way to work, cosseting herself with the prospect of seeing and touching the real thing when she's back home at night. She recognizes that her frustration with the pictures is actually a pleasure to feel, fortifying as it does the notion of a real thing. But the real thing is not real enough. Moon himself is not real enough. She wants him too much. Her appetite is unnatural. He can't possibly give more than he already does. Still, she wants everything he isn't and everything he will never be. How he exists in the negative—she wants this, too. But the contradiction is insurmountable. She can never have it; that's why she loves it; she loves what she cannot have; but she will die if she cannot have this thing that she loves not being able to have.

She wonders if she should run out of the apartment and hail a taxi to Paju. Time would pass. She would become foreign to Moon, and he to her. Only then would she return to Seoul. She would follow him around the city in secret; she would tap his phone, hack his accounts. Yes, that's it. She must become a spy. She will witness his true self only once she has been extinguished from his consciousness.

She hears Moon's footsteps coming down the hallway of the building. Can she really leave him? The key enters the lock.

The crunch of the metal has a Pavlovian effect on her. No, she'll stay. She throws her phone at the wall, disgusted with herself for accepting the halfway satisfaction of their relationship.

That night, she and Moon kiss for hours. Frustrated, she pulls away and says, "You are so good to me, thank you so much, but what's next?" Two bodies sliding up and down against each other—she's starting to see it as an act of desperation in response to the impossibility of true merging.

"Why don't we get married?" Moon says.

"But of course," Y/N says. "With enough children that I'm pregnant for a decade straight. And after that?"

"We can die together . . ."

Y/N taps her fingers on his chest with impatience.

"And after that?"

Lethargy overcomes her. Without thinking, she pushes her face into Moon's neck and kisses it everywhere, pulling the skin gently between her teeth. She feels very much at home. She occupies herself so deeply with this corner of his body that she forgets Moon is even there.

Y/N's lips are swollen at work the next day. Her morose student puts down his pen and asks if he can kiss her. She looks up in surprise at the boy. His face is already careening for hers. Y/N won't turn away, she knows this in an instant.

Guilt, curiosity, and even ambition gather into a knot inside her chest as she and her student kiss over his vocabulary workbook. Their mouths sound like radio static against each other.

She notices that her student is wearing the same deodorant as Moon, a brand that appeals to boys their age.

On her way home that evening, Y/N gets off a stop early to catch another glimpse of Moon. She stands in the back of the crowd and opens her eyes wide in the purple dusk. His neck is so bruised from last night's kisses that she cannot see where it begins and ends in the surrounding darkness. His head appears to be hovering over his shoulders. So clean was her decapitation of him that his head has yet to fall in recognition.

I WAS TRAVERSING the city by foot and feeling indeterminately ill. It was hard to breathe. My abdomen was packed with a blunt loathing of strong tastes and smells. As I followed a current of late-night revelers down a street, I was startled to see Lise, two strangers away from me, headed in the same direction. She flinched at my recognition but continued to pretend she hadn't seen me. Irritated by this thin ruse, I reached over and pulled her out of the crowd.

I cast a sidelong glance as we passed under a lamp on a quiet street. Bold geometries of shadow arbitrarily divided up her face. She kept jerking back the corners of her mouth in agitation, flashing her molars.

"I'm sorry if I scared you," she said. "But it's your own fault. You kept disposing of one place after another. I never had a chance to stay put and become a natural part of your environment. So now I'm erupting like a rude surprise."

"What do you want from me?" I said coldly.

"Don't be like that," she said. "I won't be able to bear it. Please, I want you to feel safe with me."

"Stop it. I'm not Moon. I won't help you live out this absurd fantasy."

"No," she said.

"Which part?"

"The entire spirit of it. No."

Her chin began to quiver, the skin bunching up and smoothing out with such rapidity that I worried this instability would spread to the rest of her face. She threw her arms around my shoulders.

"Oh, I'm so angry at your mother," she said, leaning her head against mine. "If I were her, I would've never expelled you out into the world, where there's nothing to hold onto and no place of certainty. I would have kept you inside my womb for as long as possible, even if that would've meant my own death."

Somehow I'd never imagined Moon as an infant. I'd also never imagined him dying. He seemed to have come into the world already complete, and I expected him to disappear in the same way.

"Inside your mother, you were perfectly round, complete unto yourself," Lise went on. "You wanted for nothing. But then you were born, and the nightmare began. Your body was pulled in all directions. Your arms, legs, neck, even your hair—they shouldn't look this way. They've been elongated by their constant attempts to reach out and anchor themselves to anything at all on the vast plaza that is the world."

I looked over her shoulder. We were standing at a major intersection. The big public clock gave the time. It was a terrifyingly specific number.

"I feel sick," I said.

"Come with me," Lise said, taking my hands. "All I want to do is cook, clean, and care for you. I won't make any demands. You don't even have to love me. Just let me be your mother."

"No," I said, pulling my hands free. "No, that won't do."

I staggered past Lise into a liquor store and squinted in the sudden fluorescent brilliance. I was jarred by my reflection in the window: the major features of my face were crassly brought to the surface, making me look like the bare minimum of myself. I slumped onto the glass counter, rattling all the neon plastic lighters out of their box. The man at the register said altogether they would cost twenty euros.

"Hey," Lise said from behind me. "What's wrong?"

I shut my eyes and tried to visualize the pain. There were bright needlepoints of shock amidst a swathe of nausea. I could see no color. The counter beneath my cheek smelled of hands and coins.

"I don't know what to do with the rest of the day," I said. "I'll go home, and then what. What do I do with all that time ahead of me. But there's also not enough time. For what, I don't know."

"It's simple," Lise said. "You find the people you love and follow them to the ends of the earth. Nothing else matters."

"But what if they turn around and spit at me. What if they make the kind of gesture people make at stray dogs." I remembered Masterson at his window. "Like they're wiping the dog off the face of the earth."

I shook with self-loathing. The man rapped his knuckles against the counter and repeated the price: twenty euros. But then I heard Korean being spoken. I raised myself off the counter and saw, on the plasma screen overhead, a news dispatch from Seoul. The Music Professor, dressed in an oversize red suit and black sunglasses, was making a rare public appearance before a crowd of reporters. In a colorless tone, she announced that Moon had retired after the boys' latest performance and that her company would be providing no further details on the matter. Then, without saying goodbye, without even a bow, she slipped into the side of a black van. The newscast cut to a clip of me in a pink cape from the party some weeks ago, taking the hands of a fan with a look of beatific generosity I'd never thought possible on my face.

When I vomited all over the lighters, the man said the price still stood, twenty euros. He was right: my insides were nothing I could pay for.

NO DETAILS FOLLOWED the news of Moon's retirement. The other boys retreated from public view and indefinitely suspended the release of their next album. Online, the turmoil was titanic. Had Moon quit of his own free will? Was he dead?

Had he relocated to the moon, surrendering himself to scientific progress and betrothing himself to metaphor?

It was around this time that I finally heard back from Masterson. But it wasn't a letter. Instead, he sent a promotional pamphlet for a company that provided therapy to people in love with someone they had "infinite in the negative" chance of developing a relationship with. The company specialized in treating individuals whose "unattainable love object" was a celebrity who had no idea of their existence.

In submission to a craven desire for some peace of mind, I decided to give therapy a try. I had a free introductory online video session with Dr. Fishwife, who was calling from his office in Los Angeles. His face hovered so close to the screen that his eyes frequently strayed out of the upper frame, leaving only his mouth in view. In isolation, his purplish lips appeared impractically ornate, like they were expressly designed to mangle sound.

Dr. Fishwife kept referring to Moon as "the recently deceased."

"I have clients in love with people who were dead from the very start," he said. "Those are the gnarliest cases. Count yourself lucky. It's easier to accept a death that happens in real time."

"Must I repeat myself?" I said. "Moon isn't dead. He retired."

"He's as good as dead. Take that mindset, and you'll recover faster."

"I can't recover on the basis of an illusion."

"Don't you understand that your entire situation is an illusion? Cases like yours are so severe that at this point all we can hope for are less severe illusions, not the absence of them."

"He might come back."

"And then what? Your chances of meeting him remain nonexistent."

Dr. Fishwife tried to look caring. I minimized the window.

"It's fine if I never meet him," I said, staring at the ceiling. "I just like the feeling of us moving through time together. I need him there. I need to know that at this very moment he's looking down at his hands somewhere in the world. It's possible that I might've figured him out all wrong, that my imagination has turned him into an absurd caricature—even then, I need to know that I'm doing all of this fallacious work in reaction to something that's real."

"You don't need him back. You don't even need him alive. Just pretend he's the main character of your favorite movie, and now this movie's over."

"No," I said. "I'm tired of experiencing reality as that which happens strictly to me. My small life can't possibly encompass all of human experience."

I could hear Dr. Fishwife paging through his notes.

"Your personal history," he said, "does indicate a high risk of falling prey to another kind of unattainable love object: the literary protagonist who commits unusual acts of willpower, frequently to his own detriment. Keep working with me, and

I can teach you how to read novels like a women's studies professor instead of a strange, dreamy child."

"I didn't read about Moon in a book. I saw him at a concert once. And there are people who've worked with him. They say he smells like grass just after rainfall."

"Exactly. He's real. So he deserves better than the feelings you purport to have for him."

"Excuse me. I never purport."

"You've settled for a comfortable distance from him so that you can yearn without suffering. Sorry, but you're not in love. You're a fan. Boring, lethargic, overfed. If you really loved him, you'd be in Seoul right now. You'd be walking the streets day and night in search of him. The magnitude of the task would crush you until you became a ball of pulp containing just your heart. All other organs—crushed into dysfunction."

I was too stunned to reply.

"The best way to fall out of love," Dr. Fishwife continued, "is to realize there exists no love out of which to fall. In future sessions, alongside a regimen of organic probiotic supplements, we can tackle the self-contempt that lies at the heart of your addiction to pursuing love where there is none and masquerading as a foreign—"

I closed out of the video session. Then I opened a map of the world and zoomed in on Seoul. I hadn't been there in ten years. I switched tabs and booked a one-way flight.

5. Real Life

VAVRA THOUGHT I'D LEFT FOR a reconciliatory getaway with Masterson. So when I called from the airport in Incheon to say that I hadn't come with him at all and wouldn't be back in the apartment for at least another month, she launched into a stern disquisition regarding my relationship with Masterson, my job, and even my upcoming appointment at the immigration office. I gazed at a lone suitcase moving round and round on a carousel, deflated by Vavra's précis of my visible life.

"Or are you there to find yourself?" she asked, suddenly hopeful.

"What?" I said. "No."

On the bus to Seoul, I sat beside a man returning from a business trip that, as far as I could tell from his phone call, had mostly perturbed him. I could hear the mollifying peeping of his wife on the other end. "I know, I know, I know," he said. "I know, I know, I know." As soon as he hung up, he fell so deeply asleep that it made me uncomfortable, like he was telling me too much about himself.

I drew aside the little curtain at my window. The proportions were startling. Row after row of perfectly rectangular apartment towers—thirty floors on average—obscured my view of a mountain range. Entire families were sitting on leather couches as high up as mountains. When the Han River appeared alongside the elevated track of the highway, I was shocked by its breadth. The river was a giant black snake with a muscular back, winding through the constructed landscape with a calm magnanimity I found menacing.

I disembarked at the foot of an overpass in Seongsu-dong. My uncle, whom I hadn't seen in years, was waiting in his car. He drove to a four-story building with a gray-tiled facade smudged by exhaust fumes. On the first floor was a restaurant that specialized in army stew, a restaurant that specialized in knife-cut noodles, a coffeeshop where one could sit, and a coffeeshop where one could not sit. In the basement was a smoky pool hall. In the corner of the building's top floor was a structure that appeared to have been added as a hasty afterthought: it had corrugated walls and was shaped like a cargo container. This, my uncle said, was where I would be staying. The studio apartment was on temporary loan from my uncle's cousin's son, who was away on compulsory military service. "Peace," I kept imagining this distant relation of mine muttering to himself as he went about his duties. "What I seek is peace."

My uncle, who worked for an electronics corporation, had to return to the office, but he came up for a quick survey of the apartment. It was June. We kept murmuring that we couldn't believe how hot it was. Incredulity seemed to be our last, but totally useless, line of defense against the monstrous power of an externality. Our mutual perspiration made us shy. We didn't know each other well, but our bodies blithely forged ahead with their self-disclosures. When he thought I wasn't looking, he bent over with a wad of tissue paper to mop up his sweat from the floor.

After my uncle's departure, I stepped out of the building for a walk, but I'd barely covered two blocks when I was accosted by a middle-aged woman.

"Your eyes are so bright," she said.

I was unsure if I should reply, or wait for more. There was nothing about her appearance that could help me deduce an intention from her words. She wore plain clothes and no makeup; she had the jaundiced aura of a long-suffering mother. I thanked her and walked on, but she joined me at my side. I noticed she had a limp.

"There is kindness in your eyes," she said. "But there is also sadness."

"What do you mean?" I asked warily.

"Let's go somewhere and talk."

"About what?" I asked, relenting again to my curiosity.

Encouraged, she grabbed my arm and tugged with surprising strength.

"Come this way. I'll explain when we find somewhere quiet."

I shook myself out of her grip and turned back for the apartment, too rattled by the encounter to continue my walk. I looked over my shoulder and saw her limping after me with an ingratiating smile, though seemingly without any expectation of catching up, which suggested she was confident she'd find me again.

I didn't see a single neighbor for the rest of the day. I only heard their rapid footsteps down the hall when they returned from work in the evening, then the smug beeps of their electronic door locks. But the man who lived directly across from me hobbled in and out multiple times with the help of what sounded like a walking stick. His tread expressed great determination, even valor. I was certain he'd been a sedulous lover in his youth. He kept his front door propped open with a large plastic tub of kimchi, facilitating the travel of cigarette smoke and the noise of the evening news all the way into my room. At one point, he blasted Beethoven's Fifth.

My uncle, who lived much farther south, called to check in. In my contusive Korean, I said the hurdles were minor but many. "I'm just very ignorant," I said in abstract summary. My uncle was appalled by this self-designation and said I should never call myself that in public. The Korean word for "ignorant" apparently sounded much harsher than I'd realized. In decades of using the word, I'd never heard it in a particularly derogatory way and wasn't sure, despite my uncle's remonstrations, that I ever would. To my added confusion, he was either shocked or baffled by my questions about the city, and he seemed to respond to them thematically without answering directly. Only after we hung up did it dawn on me that I'd been asking my yes/no questions in an intonation signaling declarative statements. Everything I wasn't sure about—he'd thought I was expressing with absolute certainty.

THE NEXT DAY, I boarded the subway at Seongsu Station, having heard about a small restaurant in Gangnam where the pack of boys had been regulars before making their debut. I stood before the double doors of the subway car. Seated to my right was a woman holding on her lap a pizza box winsomely tied with a yellow ribbon. Above her head was an ad for a plastic surgery clinic, whose patients' before-and-after pictures suggested that the ideal man should appear incapable of crimes of passion.

The train sped along an elevated track. Out the window was a sea of quadrilateral rooftops, all painted in the same vivid green, so that it appeared as though a fertile landscape had been cleanly sundered by plate tectonics. On one rooftop, a man smoking a cigarette was crouched before a line of laundry. His other hand kept a lighter flicked aflame. As a white bedsheet flapped at his back, he stared up at a continuum of pure blue, taut like a balloon, such that I felt he could raise the lighter and burst the whole sky.

When I emerged from the subway station in Gangnam, the boys began to appear everywhere, on posters and ads and screens, even on the buttons pinned onto the backpacks of uniformed schoolgirls. A dizzying array of products made use of Moon's visage: fried chicken and amusement parks, massage chairs and checking accounts, every instance of him only serving to materialize the statement "Moon is not dancing" and absurdly expecting people to pay for it. I wasn't happy to see him. On the contrary, I was scandalized by the vulgar coincidence of the cityscape with my private passion.

I found the restaurant on a quiet alley. There were no normal diners. There were only fans, sitting on the floor at low tables and taking pictures of the walls and ceiling, which were completely papered with images of the boys. I happened to arrive as a party was leaving the boys' usual table, now bolted into the floor to affirm its sanctity. Everyone in the restaurant kept taking pictures of me to take pictures of the table where the boys used to sit. I thought about covering my face to keep their photos sanitized of my pungent individuality, but they happily clicked away.

I was deep at work in my Mooncake Stew, a dish that couldn't have existed back when Moon frequented this restaurant. Floating in its spicy blood-red broth were spheres of glutinous rice cake that looked like they'd freshly buckled out of someone's joint sockets. I pretended to be Moon, unknown and disheveled, tired from practice, huddled over my bowl, but whenever I came up for air and was confronted by the wall of pictures ahead, I saw the star I'd already become.

A blue-haired foreigner suddenly sat down across from me.

"I hope you don't mind," he said in Korean. "I just want to know what it was like for our boys to sit here." He peered over into my bowl and laughed. "I knew it. I knew you also loved Moon. You're in his seat."

"You can sit here as long as you don't confuse me for Moon," I said.

"No offense, but I would never confuse you for Moon. Especially in these times."

The man affected a conspiratorial look. He was good at being redundant with his face. I asked if he was referring to Moon's sudden retirement, which, I added, amounted in seriousness to the disappearance of a country from a map. The man was gratified to confirm that I belonged to the same Moon-loving "faction" as him.

"Better enjoy this while you can," he said in a low voice, gesturing at the walls. "Rumor has it, they'll be removing every image of Moon from the city. Soon it'll be as if he never existed. That's why my team and I have pledged remembrance until the day we die. We're having lunch together right now. Join us. I like you. I like how you like Moon."

I followed him to the other side of the restaurant. His "team" turned out to be a couple, also foreigners, who were in no state to acknowledge my presence. The man and woman were sitting cross-legged facing each other with all twenty fingers knotted into a large ball between them. One would utter "Moon," and then the other would pause in contemplation before uttering "Moon"—it went on and on like this. I heard "Moon" so many times that the word began to prismatically splinter into cousin sounds.

"Moan."

"Mown."

The three of them had met on an online forum about Moon, the blue-haired man said, and when they convened in person for the first time, these two fell in love right away. Prior to meeting each other, their passion for Moon had driven away lover after lover. These former lovers, being "pagans," hadn't understood how they could be loved in parallel with Moon. The man and woman hadn't quite understood it either. Thus, romantic love up until now had been a disappointment: to satisfy a lover meant to betray Moon, which amounted to self-betrayal, leading to resentment and strangulation; as soon as one branch blossomed, another withered. But upon meeting each other, the man and woman realized they could only love someone who loved Moon. In fact, they had to love Moon more than they did each other in order to sustain the bare minimum of love between the two of them. The couple didn't even know each other's real names. All they required for conversation was the word "Moon"—by no means, however, were they calling each other "Moon," the blue-haired man noted gravely.

Moon's disappearance had been near fatal for the couple. They'd exchanged invectives of astonishing cruelty as they hung from each other's shoulders, unable to keep their balance. Without the gravitational force of Moon, the water making up their bodies had been thrown into chaos. The blue-haired man had had to intervene with a plan of action. Now the trio dedicated itself to preserving every trace of Moon's existence in preparation for the "wipeout" to come; they had several dozen external hard drives divided between their homes.

"But the biggest question remains," the man said. "Why did Moon disappear to begin with? Why did he turn his light off on us?"

In the beginning, they were, "to be perfectly honest," angry with Moon. But the three decided that if they truly loved him, they must let him disappear without demanding a reason. The task that remained was to remember Moon vehemently. But how? Friends who drifted away, lovers who broke your heart—you cared less and less about such people with each passing day. So how would you bring yourself to care more and more about someone who'd disappeared?

"Mourn," the woman in love said.

"Moron," the man in love said.

. . .

THE BLUE-HAIRED MAN said he rarely had guests. I could see why. We were alone in the bedroom of his penthouse apartment, whose walls and ceiling were covered with posters of Moon. The man walked the perimeter and rolled the ball of his hand over the pictures to make them stick harder.

"No more white walls," he declared.

This room, chaotically dense with Moon, struck me as the inevitable culmination of my day. But I newly felt that some distance was in order. His image should stand like an artifact in the chancel of a Lutheran church—a sturdy, difficult object that had slowly come into being in the shaggy environs of a belief system.

The man and I switched to English out of convenience. He said he could tell I was from the United States because the American product manager in his office had the same accent whenever she spoke in Korean. He himself was in the process of eradicating his accent, having devoted himself to becoming Korean since moving to Seoul a year ago. I couldn't tell which country he was from, and I couldn't care less. What I wanted to know was what his company sold.

"We are a global enterprise dedicated to helping the highest-achieving members of our society cultivate empathy," he answered. "Have you heard of those companies that send subscribers a basket of fruit every month? Our idea is similar.

Every month we give our clients one day in which they can pretend to be someone they absolutely do not want to be. I'm the handler who sets up the conditions under which our clients can pretend, for example, to be evicted from their home. I give them three wailing children to raise the stakes. The little girl has spots on her face, and it may be lupus. The next month, I set them up with a day of being homeless. A logical transition. We also offer a day in the life of being a cocaine addict, which a lot of our clients already are, except we also take away their cultural magazine subscriptions. You wouldn't believe what a difference that makes. We offer female clients a day in the life of having a husband who beats them. So astounded are they by the comparative gentleness of the actor who comes out of character at day's end that it's not unusual for the woman to fall in love with him. Clients rave about our program. It replenishes their well of humanity. They call their mothers. We're single-handedly responsible for a spike in donations to children with cleft lips."

The man's own lips suggested that if he had labia, they'd be parched and aloof. I wondered how he could possibly love the same person that I did. Was love for Moon a universal human emotion? Whenever someone said "I love you," were they really saying "I love Moon"?

"In any case, work has never been my priority," the man said. "The real reason I moved to Seoul is to meet Moon. Everyone tells me I'm crazy. But there's no doubt I have a better chance here than back home. And who knows—with so much time on his hands now, he might even subscribe to my company."

"I see," I said slowly. "And what would you get out of meeting him?"

"I . . . I want . . ." He fell into anxious silence. Conviction reanimated his face. "Real life. Yes, that's what I want." He walked up to a life-size plastic mannequin of Moon standing near his bed. "The height might be right. The face might be right. But this thing is a pathetic fake." He gripped the mannequin by the arm and threw it to the floor. "Yawning as I listen to Moon talk about the weather—that's real life. Not bothering to look up when Moon comes through the door— that's real life. Standing alone with Moon in a room, like this"—he grabbed my shoulders and pulled me close—"that's real life. I hope he's a truly petty and boring person at heart so that I can love him in the face of it all."

"You want to domesticate Moon," I said. "Like a dog."

"Yes," he said, misreading my tone. "After a career like that, what he needs is peace and rest."

Proximity magnified the man's features without revealing anything new. For all the emotion with which he spoke, his giant eyes struck me as dead. When I tried to take a step back, he tightened his grip on my shoulders. There was a pliability about my flesh that perturbed me. I wasn't sure why I'd agreed to come home with him.

"Don't you want to meet Moon, too?" he said. "Why don't we help each other find him? I have a map of Seoul marked with all the places he's rumored to visit undercover."

"I don't know . . ."

"You're telling me that if you had the chance to meet Moon, you wouldn't?"

"Of course I would."

"So let's find him together. Don't you think he'd like us?"

"That's irrelevant," I said, looking over his shoulder. On his nightstand was a stack of comic books with thick wads of banknotes marking where he left off last. "No, you should find him on your own. I'll only get in your way. I don't want real life. I don't even want romance. Nothing horrifies me more than the idea of marrying Moon. I need something else. Piercing recognition. Metaphysics. Byzantine iconography. I don't want to meet him; I want to have known him for years and years."

The man responded arbitrarily with a look of tenderness.

"I haven't been this close to another person's body in a long time," he said. "If we don't find Moon, at least we would have each other."

"I'm sorry," I said, twisting myself out of his grip, "but in this matter there can be no consolation prize."

Y/N'S STUDENT HAS become fanciful. He decides they will have their next session at the Gio-ji Temple in Kyoto. His parents, eager to be useful, book round-trip flights for the teacher and student. It will be Y/N's first time in Japan.

They go straight from the airport to the temple. When she sees the moss garden, Y/N thinks she might be dreaming. The color is faded, even decomposing into yellow-brown in some patches, yet the color is richer and truer than the green of a waxy leaf. The boy leads her to a gentle depression in the moss, right beside a tree. They share the depression. Sitting on her knees, Y/N unzips her backpack and reaches in for a workbook, but the boy stops her arm with a hand. Then he lays this hand on her back and gently pushes her forward until she is lying on her stomach. His hand slides up to the back of her head, which he pushes next into the moss. A macaque screeches overhead. The two humans are silent. The boy is kneeling at Y/N's side, as if teaching her how to survive a new medium to come, like water that is on fire.

Y/N parts her lips to breathe. She pushes out her tongue, prodding for soil between the thick ringlets of moss. Insects crawl up her buds, tasteless. Her eyes are open onto what can only be described as a dark intimation of green. She's so close to the moss that she can't properly observe it, but she takes pleasure in this limitation. She's tired of her freedom. There's simply too much of it. She's a small person who lives in a small room, she keeps herself small so that tremendous events can crush her into a paste. The moss hisses right back into her face. It's getting hard to breathe. She knows she's trapped in place, but she feels herself going somewhere new.

She is immersed in the moss, so she cannot see it. This is how she must know Moon. She must be immersed in him, and she must not be able to see him. Sometimes, in the skin-to-skin struggle of the sexual act, she thinks she is immersed in Moon, her vision full of dark whirling abstractions, but the lovers inevitably pull apart, and in that split second of fresh separation on the mattress, he becomes, quite strangely, that which is standing in her way to Moon. She needs a different kind of immersion, one where Moon is the world that encompasses her, where Moon is the higher idea through which all of her earthly pursuits are refracted. She must stop trying to find Moon on her plane of existence.

She shuts her eyes and twists her face out of the moss, gasping for air. The light bangs and bangs on her eyelids, begging to be let in.

Y/N returns from Kyoto seared by insight. Moon must become a performer, and she must become his fan. She must encounter him through the gigantic dimensions of collective adoration. Only then will her love be properly sized. She calls the biggest entertainment company in Seoul and gets hold of a scout there.

One evening, Y/N and Moon buy a pair of codfish and let the bodies hiss parallel in the pan until the smell fills their tiny apartment like the spirit of a third person. As the hissing dies down, Y/N realizes that Moon has been crying for the last few minutes. He's covered his face with a trembling fence of hands.

"This has to be our last meal together," he says. "I must leave at midnight to learn to dance for people like you.

I must leave at midnight to learn to become special, and you must stay as you are, unknown and unremarkable."

Y/N makes a show of magnanimity. She packs up the leftover codfish for him and says goodbye.

"It would be worse if we were to separate as two unremarkable people, lost to the crowd," she says as they hold each other on the curb. "But you will become special, even famous, so I will find you again."

When she returns home, she realizes that the third person she'd sensed in their apartment is the star that Moon is poised to become. Every human body is capable of producing a spirit that lingers apart from it. But whether that spirit is truer or falser than the body—she has no answer.

6. At the Center of the Universe

MOON'S FORMER BALLET COMPANY WAS having a performance at a theater in Seocho-gu. On my way there, I noticed a young woman approaching me from the other end of the sidewalk. I knitted my eyebrows to express quizzical aggression, but she didn't seem to notice, and it was only when she stopped right before me that I realized her eyes were directed far below my face.

"Those shoes," she said.

I joined her in looking down at my loafers, which were made of two folds of cheap white patent leather that came together at the top with a shiny buckle. I'd been forced to buy them from a man selling shoes from the back of his truck when my old sneakers had fallen apart in the middle of a walk.

The woman lowered into a crouch. She gripped the vamp of my left shoe and lifted it off the pavement. Reduced to just one foot, I nearly lost my balance and had to hold the top of her head. She didn't seem to mind. She angled her face to examine the bottom of my shoe. Dirt and choux cream clogged the trenches. She pulled from it a strand of hair that looked like it might never end. As the grotesque findings accumulated, the white patent leather acquired an increasingly strained quality.

"I've been waiting for years to run into someone wearing my soles," the woman said, looking up at me.

"What is a sole?" I asked.

Quickly intuiting my foreignness, she pointed at the bottom of my shoe.

"This part," she said. "I control the machine that shapes it. I have a job at a shoe workshop. But it'll be closing down soon."

She returned my foot to the ground and rose to full height. I thought she would never stop standing up—she was so tall. When she lowered her face to mine, I could see black flecks lodged in her light brown irises. Her black hair went down to her waist, and her eyebrows ended several centimeters too soon. She could've been either fourteen or forty. She smelled excessively good.

"How is it possible that I know exactly how your foot feels as it presses down on the sole, yet I have no idea where you're going?" she said. Her tone suggested that I should've alerted her of my plan weeks ago, when I was living on the other side of the world and had no idea of her existence.

"I'm going to the theater," I said.

"Are you meeting someone you love? Is he waiting for you?" she asked breathlessly, her eyes hard and relentless. "For the rest of the way, will you press your hand against your heart to feel it burn in anticipation?"

Moon was never waiting for me. He couldn't wait for someone he didn't know. It now seemed like such a gift, to be waited for, that I couldn't believe there had ever been people who'd waited for me, at the corner of this street at that hour, among all the possible streets and times in the world.

"Yes," I said. "He's waiting for me."

"Let me come with you," the woman said. "I want to see where my soles take you. I want to see how your life changes in them."

She followed me to the theater and bought a ticket for the seat next to mine. She walked briskly at my side and threw a vicious look at anyone who impeded our traversal of the lobby, as if my fateful reunion could not be delayed for even a second. As we took our seats in the dark theater, I looked around. Moon, of course, was nowhere to be seen.

The red curtains drew apart, and the performance began. As I witnessed the incredible grace and precision of the ballet dancers, it made sense to me that Moon had once belonged to this world. But I also understood why he'd defected: when Moon danced, he never exhibited control without intimating the threat of disintegration; he began from a position not of strength but of mortality, and this charged his movements with epic survival. But the ballet dancers were nothing more than smoothly running machines, noiseless and neoprene. At one point, a dancer fell on his side. The others didn't even flinch. The man quickly righted himself, and the troupe ossified into unassailable perfection around him. I sensed the dancers silently vowing to have nothing bad happen ever again.

As soon as the intermission began, the woman turned to me.

"Where's the person you love?" she asked.

"He's not here," I said.

"I thought he was waiting for you."

"The truth is, he doesn't know who I am."

"He might be waiting for you somewhere else right now."

"Like I said, he doesn't know who I am."

"He doesn't need to know who you are to wait for you. You must find him. When you confront him with the full force of who you are, only then will he realize he's been waiting for you. You have to show up and confront him with his destiny in the form of you."

I stared at her. She observed me unprogrammatically, without a smile.

"Is this a method you've tried yourself?" I asked.

"With you," she said.

"Look, I don't know why you're . . . like . . . gum. Sticking onto me." I was having one of those moments when my Korean couldn't keep up with my ideas. "You don't know me."

The woman's unsmiling only deepened. Yet she wasn't frowning. It was a mystery to me how she pulled this off.

"Of course I have no idea who you are," she said. "And I certainly don't know who you're supposed to be. You will be a series of unknowable people to me. My only measure of your continuity is unknowability. If I knew you, I would be tempted to use that knowledge to strike a certain effect on you. No, I don't want you to be who I think you are. Anyway, don't be so vain. I trust my soles more than I trust you. And they tell me to follow you."

WE STAYED IN our seats after the show was over. I asked her about the long scar that ran parallel to her collarbone. She tugged aside the collar of her shirt to show how the scar wrapped all the way around her shoulder. I imagined that the scar continued circling her body until it spun off like a tail. It was from when she'd been thrown off her moped. She'd asked the man riding behind her to cover her eyes as she zoomed down a familiar road, because she'd grown tired of being so used to everything. He was the last person she truly loved.

"Despite everything I've been through, I still think that my loneliness is part of some character-building prologue to the joy of togetherness that inevitably awaits me," she said. "Isn't that funny?"

I nodded sincerely while feeling no desire to laugh.

Her scar was so thick that I felt she could train it like a muscle toward athletic excellence. Beads of perspiration gleamed in the cup of her collarbone. One droplet fell over the edge, rolled down, balked at her scar, and detoured around the ridge.

"Your pain has three dimensions," I said.

"Let's get to the point," she said. "Tell me about the person you love. But please—no cold facts. What I need is his existential color. How does his body change when he hears his favorite song? What kind of games do children try to play with him when he comes around? Rant about him. I won't interrupt."

Most of what I proceeded to say was confused and vaporous, with abrupt moments of microscopic detail. About ten minutes in, frustrated by the shameful inadequacy of my words, I pulled from my backpack the box containing the thirty-day skincare regimen. The boys' five faces spanned the front of the packaging. They wore black shirts with deeply cut necklines, making the white luminescence of their skin stand out all the more. Even the whites of their eyes were not as white. I pointed out Moon.

"I've seen him before," the woman said. "He's all over the city."

"And? What do you think?"

"He looks impossible."

The box included two types of sheet masks, the first featuring aloe vera, which increased the skin's elasticity so as to widen the user's range of facial expressions, and the second featuring black charcoal, which darkened the user's face before making it whiter than ever. "You are not your dryness," the boys said in small copy on the box. "You are not your sebum." They wanted to make the world a better place, and that began with my enlarged pores.

"After I use a mask," I said, "I feel cleaner, lighter. Edited. In a month, my dead skin cells will fall away, and I'll be left with the juicier cells underneath. Then I'll be closer to who I really am."

The woman took the box and held it up to my face.

"You look way older than them," she said.

"I am not my wrinkles," I murmured.

The woman set aside for me the picture of Moon and then rifled through those of the other boys. She was under the impression that the photos depicted what could be achieved through successful completion of the program and wanted to know which of the boys she'd end up looking like. I tore open two packets, a charcoal mask for her and an aloe vera mask for me. There were holes for the eyes, mouth, and nose. She tipped back her head, and I affixed the black mask to her face, pulling at the corners so that the magical formula would seep everywhere.

We went on talking in the empty theater, though with the smallest possible contortions of our mouths to keep the masks in place. The woman told me to call her O, "like the letter." The sound constituted the first syllable of her Korean name, which she refused to reveal in its entirety. She claimed the letter O as a pictorial expression of her hope to expand from all sides into infinity, in body and spirit. When she asked what letter I would like to be, I chose N. If the two prongs of M perfectly captured Moon's bipedal stability, then N had to be me, one-legged and doddering.

"Anyway," O said in a sad voice, "what's the use of me knowing your name if you don't even have a face?"

The whites of her eyes seemed to be swiveling deep inside a charred boulder.

"Don't be fooled," I said. "There's a face under here."

"This should feel like a masked ball," O said. "This should be romantic. But frankly you look hideous in that mask. You seem to be peering out of your own face."

"When am I not peering out of my own face?" I asked.

"I'm starting to believe that the mask is a layer of skin sloughing off. Underneath you're raw. I'd have to wait for the skin to grow back and harden. Only then could I kiss you on the cheek. I guess I could kiss you on the lips right now. But maybe the lips are always raw. That's why they're pink and easy to tear."

O leaned in to test her theory. When she was an inch away, she stopped. She gagged.

"You smell like a lovely tree, but you look like an emergency-room patient who will never be the same."

WE SPED THROUGH the city in the dark of night on O's white moped. We decided to be around each other a lot until one of us stabbed the other in the back.

"But if you do, I'm sure you'll have a good reason for it," I shouted over her shoulder.

"Same," O shouted. "I'm happy that we trust each other enough to make stabbing in the back possible. There aren't many people who could stab me in the back. They wish."

I tightened my grip on her waist and looked over her right shoulder. We were still wearing the masks. In the small rear-view mirror, I could see O's mask drying and curling up around the edges, exposing her chin. But I seemed to be seeing more of her neck instead of her face, as if her face could only ever be that which hid behind the mask.

I had no idea where we were. As the moped moved at high speed toward a place where we could get dinner, the city unfolded itself with ruthless fecundity, revealing one crowded district after another, thickets of dazzling detail. When I felt O's stomach twitch with hunger under my hands, yet another plane of details, right up against my skin, entered my awareness. I understood nothing. In that moment I experienced my confusion not as a nefarious external violation—to jar and debilitate me—but as living on and through my body. The headlights on the opposite side of the road grew in intensity, but just when they seemed impossible to endure with the boiled eggs of my eyes, they abruptly disappeared. The lights repeated this process of total existence and total nonexistence.

"You are so good at moving fast," I shouted.

"Driving a moped is the easiest thing in the world," O shouted. "Keep your eyes fixed on a single point in the horizon.

Don't look anywhere else. If a truck is about to crash into you, ignore it. If a plane is falling out of the sky, ignore it. Look straight ahead and squeeze the power. Do not change course. The world will change for you. You are at the center of the universe. You can't make a single wrong move."

We wore no helmets, having decided that if the moped hit a bump and threw us off like missiles, we should simply strike the pavement and explode. As we, two masked riders, pulled onto a crowded street, people gaped at us. O brought the moped to a stop, tore off her mask, and glowered back. She looked like she'd been working down in a coal mine. Her sooty face was even further from how normal skin should look, but the pedestrians appeared relieved by the mere fact of an unveiling.

The street was lined with clothing shops and food stalls, their wares pouring out into the open. There was so much of the same thing everywhere. But when I generalized my gaze, the street became a spectacle of colorful disorder from which haphazard details emerged, including the mystical void in people's eyes during the millisecond between looking away from their friends and looking down at their phones.

I unhooked my legs from the moped and crossed the street. Lying on the ground was a life-size cardboard figure of Moon standing and waving. Propped up around him were the four other boys, manning the entrance to a cosmetic shop, all wearing pastel cardigans and white face masks just like mine. Of course, only Moon possessed the bodily dialectics to know how to stand up and lie down at the same time.

"Who's that?" O asked, coming to my side.

"It's Moon," I said.

"But how can you tell?"

Before I could stop her, she bent over, pinched the side of Moon's head, and ripped away the top layer of cardboard. Most of his face disappeared with it. Underneath, there was only brown corrugated paper. Horrified by what she'd done, O turned to me with Moon's face pinched between two fingers, unable to let go despite finding the thing revulsive. At that moment, a uniformed man emerged from the store, snatched up the cardboard figure, and threw it into the back of a box truck parked on the curb. O and I peered inside: more cardboard figures of Moon, alongside torn-up posters and greasy pizza boxes, all featuring his image.

"He's being wiped out," O said, dumbfounded. "Look, there's a Moon-themed wall calendar for the upcoming year. He's being extracted even from the future. What happened? Why aren't you allowed to see him anymore?"

"He retired," I said. "He might never appear in public again."

"So you have nothing left to love?"

"I never loved these kinds of Moon."

"Then what's left?" O insisted. "What is the right kind of Moon? You have to find the right one before they wipe that out, too."

As we sped away on her moped, I looked over O's shoulder and saw my white-masked face in the mirror. I pushed it into the crevice between O's shoulders and easily rubbed off the desiccated sheet. Once free, it whipped past my head. I looked behind me. The mask was a tiny ghost, illuminated by head-lights, buoyed by the air tunnel of machines in groaning movement. I turned back around, heaved myself up, and pressed my slimy cheek against O's. We'd decided to just order in at her place. We shouted at each other about what we wanted to eat. In the mirror, I could see our differently colored faces smashed against each other, our hair flying out as one tangled mass, our two mouths gaping in vociferous discussion. I imagined we composed one side of an invigorating debate with the black night into which we were speeding.

O LIVED ON the sixth floor of a high-rise. From the vestibule, I could see to the other end of the apartment, where there was a veranda—an enclosed porch barely large enough for a drying rack occupied from one end to the other with white sleeveless undershirts. The sliding glass door to the veranda was open. It was an odd little nook, neither here nor there: in one moment, it struck me as a creeping encroachment from the outside world, and in the next, the apartment seemed to be exiling this tiny room, slowly pushing it over the edge. Beyond, in the dark-ness, I could see the lit-up windows of the apartment building across the way, though nothing of the broader structure itself.

Cicadas were droning in full chorus. The noise swathed my senses like chainmail, delicate yet impenetrable. I could distinguish a finer pattern within the wash of noise: a nasal ascent, three short repetitions, and a buzzing falloff. Hundreds of cicadas had latched onto the trees clustered at the base of the apartment building.

"I've never lived in a place that sounds like this," I said with admiration.

"I don't even notice the cicadas anymore," O said. "I'm glutted. In fact, it's when they abruptly go quiet that I jerk awake in the middle of the night."

When we moved deeper into the apartment, we found a woman lying on a leather couch with her eyes shut and a plasma screen playing the evening news on mute. The woman wore a black shift that exposed the waxy luster of her shoulders. O sat down on the edge of the couch and lightly shook her by the upper arms. The woman's lashes, loaded with mascara, struggled to disentangle from each other as she opened her eyes.

"You've been sleeping all day," O said reproachfully.

The woman was closely watching O's mouth.

"Then give me something to do," she said. Her voice had the wobbling delicacy of a foot balancing on a rope. "Something important. I'm sorry, but I despise hobbies . . . Have you found work?"

O shook her head.

"Make sure you find good work," the woman said. "The kind of work that helps others."

"I'm not a helpful person," O said.

"I have an unhelpful daughter with a long face," the woman mused. "Sometimes I wish you'd kill someone in cold blood so that I can prove I would still love you. I would bring you Gauloises in jail . . ."

"You're falling asleep again."

O's mother stood up and smoothed down her dress. She was even taller than O. She disappeared into a bedroom. We could hear her sliding open a window. Then another. The droning of the cicadas acquired a new dimension. I had to raise my voice:

"What is she doing?"

"I'm not sure," O said, watching the door with unease. "I'm sorry, but you'll have to bear the noise. She had an accident last year, and now she can't hear a thing. But her one wish is to hear the cicadas again. It's hard to believe there was a time when she despised the noise . . . She simply couldn't get used to it. She drifted through every summer in a haze of exhaustion, and nights would pass without a wink of sleep. Now she sleeps the entire day away." O pressed my arm. "Come on, let me show you how I live."

Her room was a narrow cuboid without windows. It was essentially a hallway with a bed. Leaning against the wall were dozens of paintings in various states of completion.

"You make pictures," I said in surprise.

"No," O said. "The pictures deign to be made by me. That's how desperate they are to exist."

The largest canvas in the room was almost as high as the ceiling and composed of thick black strokes. I drew near the painting, reminded of a recurring dream in which I found myself in free fall through darkness so total, so encompassing, that I couldn't experience myself as being in movement and consequently felt no fear.

"Before I started painting," O said, "I'd spent all of my time doing one of three things: distracting myself, preventing matters from getting any worse, or obliging a person who meant nothing to me. What was I safeguarding myself for? I longed to put my life at the feet of a tremendous conviction, but not for some obvious hugeness, like a religion or a political movement. I refused to be drafted into any cause. I wanted a passion so totally mine that no one else could possibly have it. So totally mine that if I didn't exist, then the passion itself couldn't exist. I wanted a central yes."

"A central yes," I repeated. "What are you saying yes to?"

"Consider the cicadas," O said. "There's the droning of the cicadas, as a technical phenomenon of sound waves. Then there's the mystery of the noise, its vehement formlessness. Neither of these things can be painted. I paint what lies in between. When I paint, I am saying yes to something that can be neither agreed nor disagreed with."

"Your yes is a no that takes a long time to say," I said.

"Moon, backwards, begins with a long no. Moon is your central yes."

I turned away from the painting and was startled to find O standing right behind me.

"How can you be so sure?" I said. "It's strange. I think you're more sure than I am."

"Don't say that," she said. "I'm not more sure than you. I'm sure only as much as you are. I'm warning you. If you don't make good on your promise, I won't be able to look you in the eye ever again."

"What promise? Did I ever make a promise?"

"You're being disingenuous. You can't bear your own seriousness. Look at you. You're falling into a delicious languor. You like being in my room too much. I must be careful. I must alienate you. There is weakness in you, weakness from which springs the hope that I'll speak to you on the level of reason so as to rescue you from your tortured fascination."

"But what am I supposed to do? I don't know how to find Moon. I can't even be sure he's still in the country."

"In some sense, you've already found him," O said. "That's what you refuse to understand. You pretend he's somewhere else, somewhere distant from you, to avoid the greater task, and all the more difficult for it, which is to conjoin with him. Only once you recognize this can you empty your heart so that he can fill it completely."

"If I've already found him, then what is this separation I feel? This dissatisfaction?"

"It's the pain of not knowing what to do with what you've found. It's the wicked urge to control the situation, when what you must do is submit, perfectly and patiently."

"In order to see him, I have to believe," I said with sudden clarity. "I'll find him because I always knew I would. My search is but a small consequence of my conviction. All I'm doing is knocking on a door behind which he's been waiting for me."

O's mother entered the room, golden hoops shaking wildly from her lobes, as if she'd just been vigorously saying no to someone. She gestured at me to move aside. She lifted the black painting and laid it against another wall, revealing, to my surprise, a window where the painting had been. When she opened this window, the droning of the cicadas no longer simply filled up the apartment; it was a foot stomping on the side of a cardboard box and turning the whole thing inside out.

O was moving her mouth, but I couldn't hear what she was saying. Unlike her mother, who couldn't hear because she lived in a tomb-like silence, O and I were deafened by too much of the wrong noise.

THREE MONTHS HAVE passed since Moon left to train at the entertainment company. Y/N is standing in the crowd at his debut concert. Moon runs onto the stage with flushed cheeks as if called out to battle, flanked by a boy on either side. Y/N shouts his name like she used to whenever he would step off a train and fail to spot her among the strangers waiting on the platform. But now, she's not the only one calling for him, and she finds herself shouting in the same way as the others—as pure release, without any hope of recognition.

She becomes Moon's fan. She listens to his music as she packs up his old clothes for donation. She takes down pictures of them on vacation and puts up posters of Moon wearing an outfit that looks cold to the touch, like the inside of an industrial refrigerator.

When old friends call to ask if she's "all torn up" or "dead inside" after the breakup, she says no and explains why. When these friends question the prudence of trading in a real-life adult lover for a boy star who doesn't know she exists, she says, "As a human being who cannot live without love, I know full well that I have exhausted my options on this disappointing planet. The question is no longer 'Who are the people who will accept my unusual love?' but rather 'How do I make my love more unusual and more unacceptable?'"

Her friends hang up with a bad taste in their mouths.

The next day, there's a knock on her door. She's expecting her new friend O. But she finds a stranger standing in the hallway.

"It's me, Moon," he says.

She tries to shut the door in his face, but he holds it open with his shoe and sputters into nervous laughter. Y/N is alarmed. There have been reports of a madman in Seoul who seeks out women living alone and manages to convince them that they in fact know and love him. "Remember that time we kissed for so long in the dark that we started kissing our own arms without realizing it?"—specificities like that. The madman preys on women who can't tell the difference between their dreams and reality. Y/N, in honor of Moon, tells herself that she must stay rooted in reality, which is to say, in the realm of eternal distance from him. Serious fan that she is, she must not delude herself into thinking he would show up at her door and court her.

Y/N grabs the pan that's still hot from lunch and threatens to hit the man with it. He raises his hands and cries out in fear. Then he turns his face away. His quiet sobs suggest defeat. Y/N starts to feel sorry for him, this man who wants to play the part of lover so badly that any woman will do.

O comes down the hallway.

"Oh my god," she says. "He's back."

"Do you know this guy?" Y/N asks.

"Have you lost your mind?" O says, taking the man by the shoulders and pushing him close to Y/N. "It's Moon."

Disturbed, Y/N slams the door in both of their faces.

The next day, she receives a letter from the entertainment company that manages Moon, offering her a job as his makeup artist. She rejects the offer right away. She doesn't want Moon to be her job. Honestly, the idea doesn't even titillate her.

Instead, she begins a project of her own. The entertainment company recently collaborated with a toy company on a mass-produced line of Moon dolls. Y/N buys one. She lays the plastic thing on her desk and opens a tool kit. She tweezes out every strand of the doll's hair, rubs down its face with sand-paper, and strips off its clothes. Then the real work begins. Y/N plugs in new hair, chisels out a new face, and sews together a new outfit. In the end, the doll looks more like Moon than Moon does.

7. Moonchildren on Earth

ONE AFTERNOON, AS I WAS about to leave my apartment to meet O, I turned off the lights and took one last look around the room. I was struck by the crisp image framed by my window, namely of office workers taking a smoke break down below on the sunlit plaza. I had the strange feeling that I could not look out the window, that I could only look at it. The view had the flatness of a computerized reproduction.

A figure broke off from the group of smokers and drifted onto the street. It was O, hands shoved into her pockets and cigarette dangling from her lips. She had binoculars hanging around her neck. She wanted to help me find Moon.

We first took a walk along the main street in my neighborhood, where men in dirty work overalls crouched in front of their auto shops and gazed across the street at stylish young couples migrating from café to café in jeans with deliberate holes. We passed my favorite of the workers, a middle-aged man who always sat with his colleagues in the back of a pickup truck parked in front of their auto shop. His brown hair possessed incredible volume, like hundreds of little lives reaching for the sky. The hair seemed to have been lowered onto his head from above like a crown, and he never smiled, grimly acquiescent to this touch of beauty. We also passed the limping woman, who now regularly accosted me, despite my demurrals. But today she didn't even glance my way, presumably because I wasn't alone. I told O about her.

"Of course," O said. "They find people like you."

"What do you mean?" I asked.

"You've got permanent bags under your eyes," she said. "You look like you haven't slept since you were born. But the rest of your face is as fresh as a baby's. That woman thinks you've been waiting your whole life to believe in something, and she's ready to tell you what it should be."

We headed for the waterfront where Seongsu-dong was hemmed in from the south by the Han River. I led O to a vast concrete platform that sloped down into the water. Most evenings, I lay on my back on this platform as the sun set, thinking about how Moon must be somewhere to the east, west, north, or south of me.

For a few minutes, O and I couldn't hold a conversation because we were hyperventilating, taking advantage of the fact that it was one of those rare days when the city's air quality, according to our phones, was "good" instead of "hazardous." Still, I refused to switch on the air purifier in my apartment. I couldn't imagine how such a machine might work without spewing incredible toxins of its own, and I resented this extravagantly roundabout way of being killed.

"Wouldn't it be better to put thousands of air purifiers out on the street and turn them on all at once?" I said. "It's pointless to live inside a room of good air if that room is inside a world of bad air."

"This is why I respect chain-smokers like myself," O said. "I make my own body a room of bad air."

"Don't you have an air purifier in your room?"

"Yes," she said with a sigh. "Being human is like that."

I directed O's gaze westward to Namsan Tower, which stood atop a mountain some kilometers away. Everywhere I looked in Seoul, should my sight be clear of high buildings, I could see mountains in the distance. Even when I didn't see them, I knew to remember them. I told O that every time I stood on this platform late at night, when the river's perimeter could be discerned only by means of the artificial light that emanated from the surrounding traffic and buildings, I tried to work up the courage to walk all the way to the tower. If I could see it, then surely I could reach it. I would find a stranger there and lie with him at its base. A failed boxer type. As he lay on top of me, he would pummel the ground on either side of my face until the sun rose—I wanted that.

O peered through her binoculars in the direction of the tower. She lowered them.

"Well," she said. "Looks like you never made it."

O HAD A lead. Her boss at the shoe workshop had told her a strange story. According to his son, who worked as a guard at the Children's Grand Park, the sprawling venue had a lost-and-found center for children who'd been separated from their parents. The day after Moon's retirement, a man claiming to be "Moon's scraps" had turned himself into the center. The woman who worked behind the desk at the Shelter for Missing Children, as the place was called, had no idea what the man meant by this. Moved by pity, however, she provided a small heap of rice and meat every day to satisfy his birdlike appetite, and a sleeping mat, on which he nightly assumed the shape of a question mark. Most children were found by day's end and didn't need to spend the night, but the employee deemed it too cruel to send the man out onto the streets. Plus, he was the most well-behaved "child" the shelter ever had, because he was neither tearfully longing for his parents nor having a rambunctiously good time away from them. He sat without moving for hours on end.

O led us by foot to the park, whose myriad amusements, including an entire zoo, had drawn swarms of young families. The Shelter for Missing Children occupied a small building that stood just past one of the gates leading into the park. We saw the man as soon as we entered the cheerfully decorated room. He was sitting on a chair on an elevated wooden platform and staring out the window. Three children were playing at his feet with plush toys of rabbits. He wasn't much taller than them, and his arms, slim and pale, gave the impression of having sprouted recently and all at once. But he had the face of an adult; we were probably around the same age. He sat deeply hunched over with his hands gripping the edge of his seat.

I stepped onto the platform and pulled up a stool to sit across from him. When his eyes fell on my face, their irises promptly expanded. His sonorous voice made me understand his thin body as a tuning fork:

"I know why you're here. You think you've come to find out how crazy I am, but deep down you want to know what it feels like to be Moon's scraps. You're jealous."

"You may be right," I said slowly. "But please help me understand what you mean by 'scraps.' I've only ever heard the word used for the bits of food that get stuck in the drain."

"It's simple," he said. "God was in the process of creating Moon. God was unexpectedly gripped by ambition. God wasn't content to limit himself to the material usually reserved for the creation of a single person. So he reached for another pile, the bones and skin and organs that he'd planned on using for the creation of a separate being. He grabbed a handful from this pile and used it for Moon, while using the leftovers to create me."

The man was unwaveringly serious, even serene, ignoring the children as they smashed their rabbits against each other in mock battle.

"How do you know this happened?" I asked.

He freed a hand from his chair and gestured at his legs. The coarse material of his pants lay rumpled and loose on the seat as if there were no thighs within. But I could detect two small knobs of knees, barely grazing the fabric. Tucked under his chair were red plastic crutches. The man's upper body swayed precariously, hard as it was to keep his balance with one hand.

"When I was born, the doctors were horrified by the jelly-like consistency of my legs," he said. "Years later, when I came across a picture in a science book that showed a series of evolving life forms as they emerged from water onto land, I knew I was one of the creatures in between. I lived without pride for a long time. But then I saw Moon dance, and everything became clear. God had grafted my best parts onto Moon for the creation of a spectacular life. In any given pair of people, it's far better for one person to be enormously talented and the other handicapped than it is for both to be of average ability. Nothing true is ever fair. I've witnessed Moon in concert, bringing joy to thousands of people, and I knew some of those screams were for me. Now that he's gone, I think it would've been better if

God had used the entire pile to create a Moon so powerful as to be immortal, while exempting me from this halfway existence."

Cries of joy erupted in the room. A child was running into his mother's open arms. The man watched the reunion with a smile, gums fresh in exposure, his bottom teeth clustered in disorder. If he was, as O claimed, a lead, then I didn't know what he was leading me to. Should I open my arms to him? I wondered what we would do together. Would I have to endure everyone's looks of unctuous pity as I pushed him around in a wheelchair? Would I have to help him use the toilet?

"Let's take a drive somewhere," I said. "I'll order a cab."

"You can't take me away," he said. "So long as Moon is lost, I must remain here."

"What if I told you that I plan on finding Moon?"

"You would really do that?" His tone was not of gratitude but of intense hurt. "Don't you understand that he went away because he wanted to? Perhaps that's what troubles me most— that even he could no longer endure it . . ."

Another eruption of cries. More children were being found.

I didn't know what to say to the man. So I reached for his knee and hoped my grasp would convey comfort, even affection. But all I could feel of my hand was its infernal strength. As his little bone wobbled between my fingers, I had the tactile memory of wrapping my mouth around the cartilage of a chicken wing and cracking the knob apart. The man shrank back against the wall, and I was perturbed to see fear in his eyes. Perhaps what I really wanted to do was break him and send him sprawling to the floor, rendering a picture of decrepitude that would ornament with mad excess my already opulent dreams of Moon.

I withdrew my hand. The blood rushed back and diffused everywhere. My brain underwent small fits of electrocution.

I pushed the door open with O at my heels and slipped into a surging crowd of fathers, mothers, sons, daughters, and bastards. I had the distinct sense of leaving one Shelter for Missing Children and entering another. The second one was just bigger, and the children didn't know they were children.

WE FOUND THE television in O's apartment blaring at the highest possible volume. The couch was empty; O's mother appeared to be in her bedroom with the door shut. O was about to shut off the television when she froze, remote control in hand.

"Are you listening to this?" she said.

I looked up from the table where I was unpacking our takeout. It took me a few seconds to identify the painful din emerging from the plasma screen as human language. The pack of boys, a newscaster was saying, had broken their silence to announce that they would be returning "weaker than ever." Ten fans in the country would be selected by lottery to attend their first event, which was to take place, quite unprecedentedly, at Polygon Plaza, the headquarters of the entertainment company. No one knew where Polygon Plaza was, much less what it looked like. Security would be strict; contestants were required to submit copies of official identification. There was no new information about Moon, the newscaster added, but a rumor had begun to spread across the fandom that he would be making a surprise return.

"He's never coming back," I said.

It was my first time having the thought, but now that I'd had it, I was certain of its truth.

"You're probably right," O said, clicking off the television. "Still, you have to participate in the lottery."

"No. I'm so sure he'll never come back that I can't even harbor the secret hope of being proven wrong."

"That's not what I mean. I agree with you. The rumor itself proves he's never coming back. Moon can't be correctly rumored about. He sidles out of every supposition. But you have to participate in the lottery."

"Why?"

"The rumor has drawn a connection between the lottery and Moon. You must visit the site of every connection. Especially those based on a lie. You cannot leave any scrap of him hanging."

"Is that why you took me to the Shelter for Missing Children?" I asked.

I couldn't hide my irritation. O, perfectly unbothered, began unlidding one takeout container after another.

"I'm aware you're no closer to finding Moon," she said. "But this was never going to be a search where you approach him in increments. True, thousands of kilometers may have been closed between you and him, but keep thinking with a measuring stick and you'll reduce yourself to an asymptote. No, a hand must come sweeping out of the heavens. A tree laden with oranges must sprout in a chemical wasteland. You must be exactly where you need to be through a fission of bruising will-power and taut surrender. I'm trying to find new cracks for you. I won't pull you back from the edge. I will let you fall. You'll leave me for good. I've known it all along. I'm arming you with a vision that has nothing to do with me. I don't need your grati-tude, but until that day comes, can't you at least let me help in the only way I can?"

We proceeded to eat on the couch in silence. At some point, I had the uneasy feeling that I was being watched. I looked up, but the door to O's mother's room was still shut. My gaze shifted left. Through the open door of O's room, I could see a canvas lying on the floor.

"What is that?" I asked.

O stood up and walked to her room. She got onto her hands and knees, peering over the edge of the canvas as though it were a pond.

"I hope you don't mind," she said. "I'm painting you. Thank god I met you in the summer. The backs of your knees stay so smooth and white even as they travel all over the city with us. But upon closer inspection I've noticed a network of delicate wrinkles. The backs of your knees are scored with the history of your lovely movement. It makes me wonder: is perfection just the massive accumulation of small errors?"

I stood over O's shoulder. The canvas was mostly blank. In the lower half, the back of my left knee was rendered in vivid detail. Had O not told me, I wouldn't have known it was mine. I didn't know the backs of my knees well enough. Meanwhile, the back of my right knee was rendered only as a whorl of black strokes. The size and placement of the knees suggested that the painting would eventually depict my entire body.

"I'm not done yet," O said. "You're still new to me."

I was stunned by the mere existence of the painting, how O's imagination could be cracked open and pulled apart like a cervix for the crowning of such a weirdly limbed perception. I could see, even in these early strokes upon the canvas, that the work would become an image of myself truer than any reflection in a mirror. The prospect of this image—of what it might reveal—suddenly frightened me. Indeed, O's painting made me wish I could return to a time before my birth, back when I was still steeling myself for the limitations of the body to come. Then I could plan in advance all the ways in which I would dare to be. This was, of course, a pointless fantasy. I was already here, in the thick of this life, a parade of missed opportunities, a second-to-second condemnation of my mediocrity.

I got on one knee and bent over to examine the back of the other, but I couldn't see the area in its entirety no matter how much I twisted at my waist. Newly intrigued by this elusive tract of skin, I used one of the wooden chopsticks I was still holding from dinner to trace its wrinkles. I was tracing with increasing pressure, hypnotized by the unusual sensation, when the skin suddenly broke. A gem of blood burst free. O, hearing my little gasp of pain, turned around and slapped my hand away from my leg.

"It's just the back of my knee," I said. "Don't like it so much."

"You can be a real idiot sometimes," she said.

"It's my knee. I don't want it to count for anything. Don't I get to decide that?"

O didn't respond. She was busy dabbing the back of my knee with a wet tissue. So much closer was she to this part of my body than I was that the two of them appeared to be in collusion against me.

UNABLE TO STAY away for long, Y/N sees Moon in concert again. She's just as overwhelmed as the first time. Her chest tightens with panic as she remembers that Moon will be going on tour with the other boys for the next four months, leaving her no choice but to follow him around the world. She starts to wonder how many more concerts she'll have to attend before she achieves some semblance of satisfaction.

Satisfaction of what? she asks herself.

Dark blue light floods the stage. It's time for Moon's new solo ballad. He's wearing a white blouse studded all over with genuine diamonds. They weigh down the fine cashmere, accentuating the childlike smallness of his shoulders.

He begins to dance. In the middle of the song, he throws his hands into the air. Then, it transpires: the ineffable move she witnessed months ago in their apartment. Nothing about the move has changed, yet she almost fails to recognize it—perhaps it's the stage, the audience, the altered circumstances. The move sends everyone into a frenzy of euphoria; even Y/N experiences a fresh wave of joy. She's proud of him, pleased that the world can finally witness this moment of beauty. But she feels bereft as well. The move has been snatched from the secret cabinet of her joy and thrown onto the stage for all to see. She looks around in a daze. She's perturbed to witness such sweeping agreement on what was once an intensely private experience.

Moon's song hasn't even ended when she turns around and walks out of the stadium. As she heads across the parking lot in the dark, she smashes a mosquito against her ear, irritated by the woeful soundtrack of its hysterical survival.

I COULDN'T IMAGINE a better death than falling over from walking too much. One afternoon, I began at the concrete platform by the river and walked northeast through Seongsu-dong until I reached a stretch of open market stalls, which carried me past a university, at which point I made a northwestward loop that took me past Children's Grand Park and into Wang-simni, where my father had grown up.

I managed to find a modern high-rise for which, I suspected, his childhood home had been demolished. I tried to imagine my father on this plot of land, daydreaming seriously, but all I could see was the building falling out of the sky and crushing him.

I embarked on another long walk, this time to Daechi-dong, where my mother had grown up. As I wound between the residential complexes, I remembered a story. When my mother was ten, a thief had poisoned their dog in the yard so that he could conduct his burglary unobstructed. The next morning, the entire family awoke to the shouts of my uncle, who'd found the dog dead on its side. My other uncle ran out the door. My mother ran out the door. My grandparents ran out the door. That afternoon, they searched the house for what might have been stolen. But as they swept their hands across every table, every shelf, they found that they couldn't tell the difference between a space where something had gone missing and a space where nothing had been to begin with.

Years later, my mother's father, a scholar of folklore, now long dead, wrote about the incident for a literary journal. He wrote about how his son discovered the dog in the yard, how his other son ran out the door, how his wife ran out the door, how he ran out the door, how even their neighbors ran over. Not a single word about my mother. She, who had always thought of herself as most loved by him, read the essay once and never again. She had run out the door, fallen to her knees at the dog's side, and embraced it with her entire body. She had done all of these things. Or had she not? What had gone missing, the movements of her body or the love of her father? Unable to bear the disappearance of the latter, she willed herself to believe that she had stayed in bed with a fever that morning, that she had never run out that door, that she had never embraced that dead dog.

8. Polygon Plaza

O TOOK ME TO THE far outskirts of Seoul. We were alone on the sidewalk, which had the breadth of a seaside promenade but was lined with one gray industrial building after another. There was a persistent clanging in the distance and the smell of burning rubber in the air. We turned a corner and came upon a street that I could've sworn was the one we'd just left behind. But then the glittering peak of a mysterious structure rose into view between the manufactories.

What unfurled into completion was a colossal building shaped like an Egyptian pyramid. It sat in the center of an immense field of grass surrounded by industry. The building's entire facade was composed of mirrored glass reflecting the cloudy sky with such clarity that there seemed to be a perforation in the sky itself where the double doors of the entrance had been flung open. At its threshold stood a black-suited man, who was waving in our direction with impatience.

"Let's go," I said to O. "I don't think we should be here."

She grabbed my hand and pressed something into it.

"I knew you wouldn't participate in the lottery, so I did," she said. "Your pig-headedness means you'll have to enter Polygon Plaza as me."

I looked down. It was her national ID.

"Wait—"

"But now I know it had to happen this way," O said. "To protect the purity of your faith. Luck has befallen me because it knew I had no interest in using it for my own good."

Without giving me a chance to speak, she pushed me onto the grass, making me fall onto my hands and knees. I was hurt that O would handle me so, but then I realized, to my greater pain, that she was sending me away, that she wanted me to forget her in the name of my search for Moon. When I got to my feet, I saw that the man was waving more impatiently than ever. I was certain that if I took another step in his direction, I could never return to O. I swept around—she was already gone.

There was no path to the building. As soon as I began the long walk across the grass, the man's hand dropped to his side. A cloud drifted past in the towering glass facade, making the building, for all its sharp contours, appear vaporous, like it might disappear at any moment. When I finally reached the man, I laid O's ID on his outstretched hand. That was when I had my first proper look. In the picture, O had short hair tucked behind her ears, its ends curling up from under her lobes. Her real name was Oseol. The man scrutinized me, then waved me in.

The grass surrounding the building continued past the front door and sprawled into the farthest corners of the vast lobby. Sunlight filtered through the slanted glass walls and cast a spectral fog upon the indoor field. There was no other lighting, and the air was cool and fresh. So great was the size of the plaza that it took me several minutes to cross to the opposite side, where the nine other lottery winners were already gathered in tense silence before the doors of an elevator. Averse to meeting any more fans, I stood in the back beside a middle-aged man dressed for the office, arms crossed and face dark with harassment, as if he were surrounded by incompetent functionaries.

The elevator opened with a chime. Sun stepped out. Strangled noises rose from the group, and the office worker, to my disappointment, punched his own thigh in quiet victory. Sun was wearing black dress pants and a black polyester jacket filled with a thin layer of down. He bowed deeply, making the material rasp. I was startled to see gray streaks in his hair. He rose, paused, then rushed forward with a smile and began shaking our hands.

"I know this might come as a shock," he said as he moved through the group. "But I thought it best to get our meeting out of the way, without any fanfare."

He gave my hand a superficial squeeze with his face already turned to the office worker. When the man's turn came, he would not let go of Sun's hand.

"Please," the boy said with extreme gentleness. "You'll ruin it for the others."

The office worker looked around at the rest of us with distaste. Then he let go. Sun remained standing at the man's side in seeming assuagement and continued speaking:

"Welcome to Polygon Plaza. The boys and I are so pleased to have you here. I know—you're probably wondering where the others are. Don't worry, they're in the building, tucked into their favorite corners, getting ready to meet you. But you will be alone with me for the first hour. It's easier that way, for there is much to explain. Plus"—he smiled knowingly—"you know what I'm like, don't you?"

There was a beat of silence, then someone called out:

"You're the boss!"

It was a chic elderly lady with an easy air about her. The group relaxed into laughter. Sun joined in, shaking his head in self-deprecation.

"But I've gotten better over the years, haven't I?" he said. "Remember how merciless I could be with Jupiter? And he causes me no less trouble these days."

"You really did have an awful temper back then," the elderly lady said. "I always admired Mercury for trying to fight back. Moon, however, would fall into a catatonic state that resembled my late sister's—"

Sun raised a hand, cutting her off. A fearful hush fell over the group.

"Let's move on." He swept his hand to the side. "Polygon Plaza has ten rooms, each of which occupies an entire level of the building. Here we are on the first floor, which, as you can see, has been overtaken by the outside world. The boys and I must never forget the world. We must feel it grabbing at our heels, trailing in after us, even as we've reached the seemingly safe shores of Polygon Plaza. Only with a fresh awareness of the world's dangers can we stand on the other floors with the urgency required to create work of any significance."

Sun pressed the button for the elevator, opening the doors.

"Or so we thought. That was why we never invited you here. We sought seclusion in our own small society so that our work would be bright and strange. We felt that we couldn't be in the world at your side if we wanted to touch you at the deepest level of your souls, for we weren't your friends, no, we were agents of upheaval. But everything has changed since you last saw us. Now we need you here. So please, step inside."

The back wall of the elevator compartment sloped in conformity with the building's pyramidal architecture. We had to pack ourselves close to the door, beside which was a single column of ten square buttons.

"No curves are to be found anywhere in the building," Sun said. "Even the light bulbs are cubes. As the Music Professor likes to say: 'Let the corners stab.'"

Without trying, I ended up standing next to Sun. On the other side of him hovered the office worker, who continued to survey the rest of us with gloomy superiority. He was like a father and a son at once, protecting Sun while also petulantly demanding his attention. None of this escaped the boy, who rested his hands on my and the office worker's shoulders in a show of impartiality. So uninvested was his touch, lacking even in the tension of restraint, that I grew attuned to the slim void between his fingers and my shoulder. When he lifted his hand away to press for the fifth floor, what I experienced wasn't freedom but a crushing density of air.

WE DISEMBARKED INTO a dark, musky library. Shelves of books wound through the room in a disorderly line, not unlike intestines, creating uneven amounts of space between the shelves. A small golden lamp was affixed to the head of each shelf, illuminating its contents, which were organized not by author or title, but rather, we were told, by the first word of the text.

The sole exception was the section devoted to the dozens of volumes of social critique authored by the Music Professor. Sun led us to the shelf, which was built into the center of one of the sloping walls. The Music Professor knew nothing about music other than its capacity to move her deeply, and she intended to keep it that way. But she was an expert on the Himalayas and the Galapagos, she knew how to speak Russian and

Turkmen, and she knew how to break bread with the very poor as well as the lofty elite, having led, until founding the company at the age of forty, a richly nomadic life, the details of which remained obscure to the public. She had given herself the title of Music Professor with irony, Sun said, for nothing revolted her more than the modern university. She considered it a clinic of castration for minds as well as the sexual organs; nowhere did you find dumber, unsexier people. Whenever the boys sought her advice, she directed them to a book that bore no relevance to their problem. Whenever they asked her a question, she responded with at least ten questions in turn.

"Have you been reading as if your life depends on it?" she liked to ask the boys. "Have you been reading as if every single sentence could be true? So that as soon as you build an affinity for the ideas of one book, another book comes along with ideas of its own, and as soon as you think it's one versus the other, dozens of other books appear, parts of some aligning with parts of others, sowing confusion in your soul? Have you been reading until you feel sick on everything you know?"

In the corner of the library was an acne-ridden young man sitting with his feet propped up on a baize-surfaced desk. We gathered around him, but he made no move of acknowledgment, too immersed as he was in a massive tome spread across his thighs. He had just paused on an image in which a breast and an eyeball were inexplicably the same size. Sun laid a hand on the back of the young man's chair and introduced him as the librarian. Because the Music Professor wanted the boys to cultivate diverse intellects, rare was the item that failed to make the shelves. There was just one criterion for rejection: any direct reference to the boys. Under the librarian's strict surveillance, not a single biography, reportage, or scholarly work about the boys could penetrate the walls of Polygon Plaza. The Music Professor insisted that the boys be masters of their own identities. No one in the company, not even the makeup artists, was permitted to watch a boy gaze at his own reflection in the mirror. He possessed the inviolable right to contemplate his own image in private, insulated from how others conceived of his relationship with himself.

The boys would remain the Music Professor's sole project until she retired. She released—without any questions asked— whatever they made. She never told them what to do. Freed from the obligations of school, family, and money, the boys had that which all artists dreamed of: time, endless time. Plus: musical instruments from all over the world; the country's largest collection of records; various rooms in which to practice; and a recording studio featuring hundreds of buttons, dials, and switches for the infinite manipulation of sound. All of these resources could be found on the other levels of the building.

Consider how few genuine incursions creativity made into the average life, the Music Professor often said. What would happen if creation were a job to do? Culture amounted to a collection of agreed-upon values that made it possible for large groups of people to live beside each other in relative peace.

What would happen if a teenage boy shared a culture not with billions of strangers but with just a few other boys? What would happen if context, especially the crass pressure of survival, were stripped away? What would happen if physical security, creative fulfillment, and even wild success were guaranteed? How might a boy construct his humanity outside of these aims?

But nowhere on the planet was there room for this kind of experimentation. Too urgent was the basic task of survival for the poor. Too stultified were the well-off by shame and hypocrisy, by their spineless parroting of the propaganda they confused for higher learning. This was where the Music Professor made her intervention. Polygon Plaza cordoned off space for a certain kind of experience that was becoming ever rarer in the world. She liked to compare Polygon Plaza to a monastery: a place where the dissolution of the self produced moments of astonishing self-expression.

In advanced societies all over the world, people were running around in circles and indulging their small adorable freedoms, like wearing this or that outfit or sleeping with this or that person. They confused their navigation through the stunning variety of meaningless choices as an expression of their individuality. True individuality, however, was indistinguishable from the evacuation of the self in service of a higher purpose, she claimed. At first glance, this self-annihilating devotion might seem to produce a peculiar blandness of character. But look deeper, she urged. The true individual abstracted his personal desires so as to perform bold acts of creation or faith. He took the dense yet limited substance of his lived experience and charged it—through sacrifice, through discipline—with breathless latitude. His work was thus capable of setting the souls of others on fire.

So the problem with today's cultural excretions, according to the Music Professor, wasn't the erosion of an artist's idiosyncrasy but the insufficiency of that erosion. This was not limited to the arts. The spiritual vacuity of our consumption and conversation, the daily torture of justifying our ethical fraudulence, the ever intensifying yearning for love in a world that systematically handicapped our very capacity for it—amidst this desolation, how could one not think that the solution was to retreat behind the walls of the self and become utterly singular? This was why people clung to markers of identity as if they were differentiating, when the mere fact that there already existed a name for this difference meant it wasn't differentiating enough. No, the perverse cunning of the human spirit manifested itself in submission to the erosion of all categories, a descent into namelessness, homelessness, nothingness. Only then did one have a chance at achieving universality.

A STRANGE MALAISE had fallen upon the group. Eyes had glazed over by the end of Sun's monologue. Back in the elevator, he pressed for the seventh floor.

We disembarked into a rehearsal room, which, after the density of the library, was strikingly bare, as if to drive home all that the boys could do with just their bodies. The four walls were paneled in mirrors. We remained by the elevator as Sun went ahead and roamed the space with his head lowered. In the glass, infinite versions of himself fell deep into thought.

He turned to us with abrupt resolution:

"It's good to have you in this room with me. The truth is, the other boys and I haven't been here in a while. Strange impulses have befallen us. We leave Polygon Plaza and wander the city for hours to press our hands against its hot concrete. We crave the truth of an easy sensation. We want to fight and desire, to have favorite things. We want the heavy fist of the world to press down on each of us and crystallize a personality into being. But everything remains at a distance. We don't know how to meet the eyes of a stranger on the street. We don't even know how to enjoy the weather. We're a nail that keeps slipping out of the wall; we can't stay involved. Having lost our primal instinct for life, we no longer have one for art."

A young woman broke out of her sluggishness and stared at Sun with indignation. How dare he bore her, so much so that she should forget to be astonished by his presence? A shadow crossed Sun's face as he realized that the group was failing to grasp the urgency of his words. He raised his voice:

"We once treated the Music Professor's ideas like holy law. But now we wonder if she might have been wrong. You see, we've spread ourselves too thin. We don't know how to reach you anymore because we don't know where we're starting from. This is why we've decided to open Polygon Plaza to you for the next six days. You may visit every floor except the tenth, from which even the boys and I are forbidden. Roam free, create at our sides—and pump us with the gasoline of your experiences. Tell us who you are. Tell us how one lives. Everything you share with us—we will express it in a unified work of art. The other boys will be joining us soon. Venus is excited to study your faces—'like Greek sculpture,' he said. And Mercury has fallen silent to conserve his words for all that he must say to you . . . Anyway, let's drop the honorific and speak freely with one another. We are now peers in art, after all. Go ahead, make yourselves at home."

I took a step back, feeling as if a bowl had dropped face down on the cockroach of me. Murmurs of excitement had broken out, and a few people seemed on the verge of anxious tears. But the office worker remained as stony as ever. He broke free from the group and took a step in Sun's direction.

"I was afraid it would come to this," he said. "I've been watching you for the last year, just you, my boy. You're simple; it's the beautiful truth of your character. Your fancy talk and charitable whims—they pain me with their falsity. And now you've really done yourself in. Why don't we step aside and have a talk about your future? You need to be careful here. Don't let these people put their dirty hands

all over you. Who knows, they might be criminals, prosti-
tutes, animals—"

I escaped into the elevator and pressed for the tenth floor.

I STEPPED INTO a small room with a sweeping view. The
room was identical in shape and size to the elevator compartment I'd just exited; together they formed two halves of a
pyramid. I needed to take only a few steps before I could
press my forehead against a sun-warmed wall of glass. I was
standing at the tip of Polygon Plaza.

I could see the world for kilometers ahead, and none of it
was beautiful. Dozens of apartment complexes, all of the same
dimensions and same shade of gray, thrusted out of the ground
like stiff barbs of hair. I was observing from such a height that
the buildings, spread across the landscape in precise rows,
looked as if they were standing at my command. Beyond
these buildings was an industrial power plant. There were
three smokestacks. At their base was a structure of scaffolding
spangled by liquid points of light. As with the apartment
buildings, the presence of humans was unquestionable, yet not
a single person could be seen. From each of the three stacks
emerged a column of smoke that subsequently collapsed to
the side from its own weight. The smoke thickened along the
way, darkening in color, gaining bold contour. It replenished
itself with vigor. All that moved in the landscape was the

smoke. And yet there was something undead about the emission, lacking as it did a clawing desperation to survive, as well as the unpredictable outbursts of cruelty that accompanied the cycles of nature.

I swept my gaze across the apartment complexes. Then something moved. An arm was jutting out from the top floor of a building, its hand swinging lazily at the wrist. Almost as soon as I saw it, the hand stopped moving. Then it vanished. I imagined it gliding away from the window into a dark room. Perhaps it was now doing the dishes or ironing a shirt. Inside all of these bulwarks of metal and concrete, I realized, hundreds of hands were opening and clenching, hitting and grazing, yearning to land upon a gesture of beauty, like that of a dancer. But then I pictured the buildings falling apart and disgorging these hundreds of hands, all of them grasping for something to hold onto but finding nothing but air.

I pulled away from the glass, electrified by the conviction that Moon and I were finally in the same place—not Polygon Plaza, not even Seoul, but a place of far greater dimensions, an incalculable realm of possibility where encounters between individuals were rich and oxidizable like the gashed flesh of a peach. I could feel him there, thrumming at a distance, roaming the same wilderness as me, a fellow exile without a map. I was finally in the right place. But this place, precisely for being right, was the most daunting yet, and easier to lose my way in.

. . .

I HEARD THE elevator open behind me. I yielded in silence.

Inside the compartment, the black-suited man pressed the top and bottom buttons at the same time. They blinked twice in enigmatic assent, then the elevator glided all the way down, past the lobby of Polygon Plaza and into the earth.

I stepped out into a chamber so large that I couldn't perceive its distant limits. It was divided into large sections, each illuminated by a hanging lamp, between which lay wide strips of darkness. I found myself standing inside a small rectangle of light, occupied only by a hatstand, on which hung a black leather trench coat. Just up ahead, I could see the Music Professor sitting behind a desk in an oversize blue suit. Shelves of books towered at her back. To the right was an illuminated section featuring a four-poster bed; to the left was a kitchen. This underground chamber, I realized, was the Music Professor's apartment, one without any walls.

She gestured at the chair on the other side of her desk in invitation. I crossed out of the foyer and into her office.

"It's nice up there, isn't it?" she said. "As a child, I dreamed of living in an attic room and reading books high over my family's heads—to be very much away. The room on the tenth floor is the belated realization of my dream. Without that room, Polygon Plaza would not exist. In all matters of my life, I design from the top down."

She propped her arm on the table and laid the side of her head on her hand. There was no makeup on her face, and she composed it utterly without tension, though the features themselves were biting and sharp—she was an empty firearm. Sustained exhaustion was legible in the wrinkles sprouting from the corners of her eyes, but they had a peculiar charm, a simultaneous delicacy and rigidity, a relaxation into her own contradictions. I sensed she always asked directly for what she wanted and had emancipated herself from the humiliation of rejection.

"You interest me," she said. "Why did you leave the group?"

Her voice wasn't unfriendly. I knew it would be pointless to speak without total candor.

"I don't want to collaborate with the boys," I said.

"But you must be a fan. Why else would you have participated in the lottery?"

"I'm looking for Moon."

She lowered the hand that had been supporting her head.

"Ah," she said sadly. "You love Moon. But tell me. Might there not have been a chance of meeting him in the rehearsal room? You must've heard the rumors."

"I never believed them. I know Moon isn't coming back. The other boys are finished; there's no hope for them. Moon would never consent to a project like that."

"Such a collaboration would indeed be out of the question for him," she said with gentle surprise. "Moon cannot compromise. But neither does he know how to make demands of others. His work is much more subtle. By simply existing at their side, he functioned as a chemical agent that intensified each boy's most spiritually independent quality. This created those deep lines of friction only out of which a philosophical unity among individuals can be born. But now, without Moon, the boys have fallen back apart into discrete talents."

"You love Moon, too," I said.

"Not like you do," she said. "It's different. There were so many hours. So many cryptic turns. He could be exacting. He was in conscious possession of his former lives and sought to reconcile them in the slim envelope of his present. He single-handedly changed the direction of my work. He drained me. There were times when I refused to let him into my office. Can you imagine that?"

"No. But I want the challenge. To love him anew. Every time."

"I no longer have the energy for that," she said, leaning back in her chair. "There was a time when my anger alone could wrench me out of bed like a hand. Now I surround myself with the boys because they are so much stronger and so much more beautiful than me. They are my energy broken into magically complete pieces. But now they're petering out, my little stars. I can't even remember the last time they visited the room on the tenth floor. Moon, however—he went up there every morning until his last."

"Sun said the boys were forbidden from visiting the room."

"That's a curious way to put it," she said with a gleam in her eyes. "No, my rule is simply this: They must be summoned to the tenth floor. They must feel as if they had no choice in the matter."

"What's supposed to happen there?" I asked.

"That does not fall within my purview," she said firmly. "Each person has their own way of receiving that which comes down. Or of reaching for that which stays above. Who can say which it is?"

Silence fell between us. Her last words were echoing in a remote corner of the room. I was certain she lived here alone.

"There's something I still don't understand," the Music Professor said. "You said you're looking for Moon. But if you knew he wasn't coming back, then why are you here at Polygon Plaza?"

"I don't know where he is," I said. "All I have are the places he used to be. But I know I will find him. Something happened when I was on the tenth floor. I felt myself leaving one place and entering another. Moon is in this other place, too. I'm sure of it."

She narrowed her eyes at me.

"Strange," she said. "You look like him. But there are so many people in the world that I suppose it's only reasonable to expect a few hundred of them to look like Moon. You look like him in a sad way." She reached over and lifted the dead ends of my white hair. "Look. Your hair is crying out for help." She flicked crumbs off my sweater. "And have you been munching on crackers? Have you ever met a cracker that's slimming? I think it would've been better for you not to look like him."

"He succeeds where I fail."

"You know," she said in a hard voice, "he's just a person, out in the world."

I sat up straight. It was my first time hearing anything about Moon's location.

"Where in the world?" I asked. "Please take me to him."

"Don't you see how lucky you are? You don't know Moon, so you think you could know him. Because you've never met him before, he's always waiting for you in a state of existential integrity." Her exasperation was wholesale, beyond me. "Sometimes I think it would've been better for Moon to have never been born. Then he would still be possible. Then he wouldn't be all used up."

"I don't want integrity," I said. "I want difficulty."

The Music Professor was silent for a few seconds.

"Show me your ID," she said.

I handed her O's card.

"So you didn't always look like Moon," she mused. "Have you had some work done? Nothing to be ashamed of. It's a good idea."

She removed a piece of paper from the inside pocket of her jacket and held it out to me.

"This is Moon," she said.

I took the paper into my hands. It was an ultrasonic image. How had I never thought to hang posters of Moon's insides on my walls? I found the proportions, however, completely illegible. I couldn't tell which part of his body I was looking at. Were this image to serve as a map, Moon was likelier to lose his way inside his own body than in a foreign city.

When I tried to return the picture, the Music Professor held up a refusing hand.

"Bring it with you later," she said. "There's little else I can give you that would help identify him."

I could say nothing.

"I'd kill to feel what you're feeling," the Music Professor said, laying her head back on a hand. "That doorway feeling. To be on the cusp of experience. I'd kill to know it again. The truth is, I wouldn't be surprised if you eventually found yourself wishing you'd stayed at Polygon Plaza instead."

"What do you mean?" I asked uneasily.

She shut her eyes.

"It's just so much better in our heads," she said.

And then she went far, far away.

9. The Sanctuary

THE BLACK-SUITED MAN DROVE ME away from Polygon Plaza at breakneck speed. When I asked where we were going, he ignored me and turned up the radio. A woman, phoning in over a crackling connection, told the host she was ashamed to see all the shoes lined up in her vestibule, for none of them belonged to a man who loved her.

We wound through a small city blighted with dilapidated buildings, then broke free onto a deserted road. More than an hour passed without any sign of human life. As the car rumbled up a grassy slope, bringing into view a lake bordered by verdant mountains, I realized with exhilaration that nature refused to consort with the wrong kind of Moon. There was nowhere for his visage to reasonably hang, nothing for him to advertise. The landscape was emptying itself of his image, sweeping away every cheap reproduction in anticipation of my arrival. I couldn't be far now. Amidst the clean shock of grass, I would find him standing there, protruding with insolence, whole unto himself.

The car pulled up in front of a two-story house constructed of interlocking wooden beams, with a curved black-tile roof and a stone turret—it looked as though a hanok had been stretched in all directions to assume the grandiose stature of a Victorian estate. Waiting on the porch was a middle-aged woman wearing a forbidding expression. Yet another person standing between me and Moon, I thought with icy determination as I climbed the steps. But this stranger hugged me as if we hadn't seen each other in years.

"How could I not admire you?" she said. "You came all the way here for love."

I was too startled to speak. Aggravated by her floral perfume, I tried to wriggle free. But she would not let me go. Suddenly overcome by exhaustion, I sank into her bosom with relief.

"I rarely allow visitors to the Sanctuary," she said. "But I made an exception for Moon, and now I'm making one for you."

Even as the woman pulled away, she kept our bodies close, draping my shoulders with her hands, which seemed to need a lot of rest, freighted as they were with complex rings. Her hair, dyed a violent hue of red, was coiled high atop her head, and the silk of her tight-fitting dress sighed with every move of her plump body, as if lamenting the existential precarity it had to endure in the name of abetting her beauty. She was impossible not to gawk at. In any case, she liked the attention, gamely following my eyes as they traveled down her dress.

"Is he expecting me?" I asked.

"I haven't said a word. The slate remains clean. An arena in which to play out your fantasies, the chance to corner at last the elusive gazelle that is the beloved—this is all I can provide in the way of assistance."

"I understand," I said with a firm nod. "If everything goes wrong, there should be no one but myself to blame."

"That's the spirit," she said, stroking my face. "You're trembling like a foal. Has no one touched you in a while? Don't be embarrassed. Being practiced at love is exactly what ruins it."

Then she extricated herself with delicacy and slapped me lightly on the cheek, as if to say enough was enough. Had she pushed me around some more, I wouldn't have minded. I knew there wouldn't be a woman like this for another hundred years.

"Ready?" she asked.

"Of course not," I said.

"Me neither." She inhaled sharply, eyes stricken with ineffable emotion. I had to wait a worrisomely long time for her to breathe back out. Composure regained, she sashayed for the front door. "Stay close. It's easy to get lost around here."

I followed her into a tastefully decorated sitting room. Moon was nowhere to be seen. Instead, there was a white-haired man so severely hunched over in a wheelchair that I couldn't see his face. He was breathing with mammalian furor, making the wheels squeak back and forth on the floor. Resting on a chaise longue beside him was an old woman with cartoonishly drawn eyebrows, the black lines careening past her temples, as though she'd been angry with herself as she'd stood before the mirror that morning. She stared ahead, slack-jawed. The couple, if they were one, did not acknowledge our entrance. No conversation was underway.

"What's wrong with them?" I said.

"I beg your pardon?" the proprietress said. "There's nothing wrong with my patients. Through no fault of their own, they've become children once more. People look to the future and imagine meeting their soulmate or traveling to France, but do they ever imagine having dementia?"

She went on to explain that three demented patients lived here under her care. The Sanctuary, neither nursing home nor medical clinic, skirted the boundaries of legal propriety for a number of reasons, the foremost being that the Caregiver, as she called herself, had never received formal training in this line of work. Moreover, she refused to install the pertinent medical equipment—"no style," she said, "and no fun at all." True, her patients could probably eke out an extra year hooked up to the high-end gadgetry of a university hospital, but the Caregiver knew, at the bottom of her heart, they wouldn't feel even one percent as loved as they did here.

"In the short time they have left, I hope my patients enjoy the small but intense paradise I've created for them," she said. "For maximal sensory pleasure, I blast the air-conditioning but keep the floorboards heated from below. My patients eat like kings. Tonight it's lobster tail. I'm also fond of organizing unforgettable activities. I've seen Miss Lina on a horse . . ."

She began to fuss over the man in the wheelchair, fixing his collar and smoothing down his hair. I still couldn't see his face, but a strand of saliva was slowly elongating from his chin. I wondered if this was a message for me, the viscous leakage of his otherwise incommunicable thoughts.

"Moon," I croaked. "Is that you?"

The Caregiver turned to me with a sharp look.

"I know love can play tricks on the eyes, but please keep my patients out of your delusional episodes. This is obviously Mister Goun. He couldn't be someone else if he tried—so inimitable is his soul." She raised her voice: "Isn't that right, Mister Goun?"

The decrepit man unfurled himself with dinosauric effort. His face was carved with wrinkles from top to bottom. He must have spent his life passionately emoting; so much love and injustice must have come his way. As the Caregiver bent over with a handkerchief to wipe the spittle off his chin, she had her lips pursed as if requesting a kiss. Here was a woman who seduced willy-nilly. She did not make discrete advances on individual men; her life was one prodigious advance, and only death could turn her down. Once finished with the handkerchief, she tucked the soggy thing into the lacy cup of her bra.

"Mister Goun, do you know where Moon is?" she asked.

"I want to know," he murmured. "But I really don't."

At the sound of burgeoning activity, the woman on the chaise longue rustled to life. She was so thin, I could've mistaken her for a single tibia swaddled in cotton. She appeared incapable of making any kind of impact on the world.

"Moon?" she piped up. "Who the hell is Moon?"

"Miss Lina," the Caregiver said reproachfully. "Let's see how well you keep your cool once Moon comes around. I saw the way you were sitting in his lap last night and making yourself comfortable."

The Caregiver took the handles of Mister Goun's wheelchair and beckoned all of us out of the room. I followed at her heels in bewilderment.

"But why is Moon here?" I asked.

"All I know is he needed a place where he could live in peace and quiet," she said with a shrug. "The Music Professor has an uncanny sense of people, of what they're capable of giving one another. She knew I would leave him to his own devices, not least because I couldn't care less about all that dancing and singing and whatnot."

She gave Miss Lina a spurring pat on the back, then turned to me with a look of grim disapproval.

"On that note, I have to admit I don't understand how you could've fallen for a celebrity. We're no longer at the age for such things, are we?"

THE CAREGIVER LED us down a corridor that went on and on, until I found it impossible to correspond the Sanctuary's sprawling inner dimensions with the house I'd observed from outside. Space seemed to be proliferating from within. Over our heads, torrid pansori was playing at low volume. This flourish gave the Sanctuary the mannered drama of a history museum—the history of what, I could not say.

Like the Music Professor, whom she'd known since they were schoolgirls, the Caregiver had completely changed the direction of her life a few years ago. Prior to opening the Sanctuary, she'd been a blithely unoccupied housewife with a "whorish appetite" for her own husband. "Happy decades," she summed up with a frown. But then his mind had started to go, and she'd been forced to watch as the vast history of his humanity attempted to push itself through a tiny hole in the wall, only to emerge as a degraded paste. Worse yet, his illness guaranteed him the minimum sliver of consciousness necessary to recognize, on his dying day, just how badly he'd lost the game of his own life.

"My aloneness in the world has extended my heart into strange places," the Caregiver said. "I really had no choice but to create the Sanctuary—it's the magnum opus of my life, one that I've dedicated to emotional nepotism. I must have received some ten thousand applications, documenting dementia in all its harrowing colors, but I chose my three favorite cases and threw the rest into the trash. Now that Mister Goun, Miss Lina, and Mister Suguk are here with me, they shall be the sole recipients of my devotion for the rest of my life, and I will never have any others."

Being old was already bad enough, she said, but add to that an unruly mind, a roguish creativity, and one wound up like her patients—lumpy, ugly wreckage left to rot on the shores of an increasingly polyester culture.

"Everyone wants to take, but no one has anything to give," she said. "People are craving touch, sensation, depth. But nobody can feed them, for the same people they beseech are busy beseeching someone else. The world: a chain of beseechers. I've extracted my patients from this vicious cycle. I organize the world in their favor. I infuse their lives with energy in excess so as to offset the draconian imbalance they've had to suffer for too long."

I started at the touch of a skeletal hand on my arm. I turned to find Miss Lina's vacant gray eyes in alarming proximity.

"Have you heard from my younger brother?" she asked.

"I'm sorry, but I have no idea who your younger brother is," I said.

"I must find him. I must go right away."

She turned aside to split off from the group, only to confront a wall.

"Well . . . where is he?" I asked.

"I put him down because my arms got tired. I lost sight of him after that. There were too many people around. All of us were in a hurry to get away. Everything would be different if I'd had better arms . . . Are you sure you haven't heard from him?"

"I—"

"Miss Lina," the Caregiver interjected. "Why don't you lead the way ahead? Miss Oseol is new around here."

As the old woman hobbled down the corridor, the Caregiver explained that Miss Lina had begun speaking of this "younger brother" when her mind had deteriorated beyond recognition. Strange how it was only when she lost her grip on the most quotidian facts that she remembered the one thing she'd spent her entire life trying to forget. Her husband and children had never heard about this brother before; they couldn't even be sure he really existed. Not that their opinion mattered. They hadn't visited Miss Lina a single time, the Caregiver noted tartly.

The corridor finally opened onto a circular antechamber with three doors—rooms where the patients could do "whatever they want." The Caregiver thought of these spaces as "ateliers," cracks in a desiccated modern landscape through which her patients bloomed like wildflowers. Out in the world, her charges were called demented; here, they were lauded artists.

She led us inside Mister Goun's atelier. The walls were pinned with pencil sketches he'd made of some unidentifiable and protuberant object, repeated with minor variations. Had it not been for the Caregiver's elucidation, I would've never guessed they were stiletto heels. Mister Goun could no longer draw a straight line. But things had been different back in the day, when he'd been a much sought-after shoe designer who knew how to give women the pleasure of feeling their legs lengthen out below them. He used to say that his ideal clientele were "haughty ladies": transformed by his creations into beautiful but teetering buildings, they would yield at last to their true desires and crumble strategically into the right masculine arms. This had been Mister Goun's way of engineering love stories all over the world.

I watched as the old man wheeled himself over with surprising vigor to a glass case displaying his latest design, which the Caregiver had specially ordered for manufacture. The shoe slumped in distortion—its heel was a woeful stub, its sole four times too broad.

"Want to try it on?" the Caregiver asked. "I think it would look good on you."

"It will make me fall," I said forlornly, "and into no one's arms."

Back in the antechamber, we found Miss Lina walking in circles, looking around as if she sensed something in the air.

I cast the Caregiver a questioning look, but she hushed me and pressed her ear to the second door.

This atelier belonged to Mister Suguk, whom I had yet to meet. He was "rather kooky" even for a demented person. It was hard to say what was his dementia and what was him—or perhaps he'd been demented from the moment of his birth? "Could be," the Caregiver mused with affection. By the end of his thirties, he'd failed to publish a single one of his poems and was twice divorced. He eventually resigned himself to working as a geography teacher at a high school, where he became infamous for his "unusual" lessons.

Mister Suguk's work continued at the Sanctuary. Every morning, he showed up to his atelier and waited for his students to arrive. The cornerstone of his pedagogy was the requirement that every student strike up a long-term written correspondence with a peer in a foreign country. There were no parameters regarding the content. All he asked was that his students never exchange pictures, never arrange a phone call, and certainly never fly out to meet their pen pals. In class, students were required to read aloud every letter they received. It was best to leave Mister Suguk undisturbed, the Caregiver said, stepping away from the door, unless we were prepared to present the latest findings of our "research." The old man did not take this exercise lightly; it was no children's game. He expected his students to be transformed by their "spiritual correspondents," these "alien visitations." What all of this meant exactly, the Caregiver could not say—personally, she found his lessons difficult to sit through.

"In ancient times, Mister Suguk would've been a bard renowned throughout the kingdom—a consequential personality," she said. "But what is he in this day and age? Nothing."

The Caregiver moved onto the third and final atelier. When she opened the door, materializing a slim column of brilliant light, Miss Lina pushed us out of the way and slipped through the crack with liquid inevitability.

HUNDREDS OF CHERRY blossom trees were at peak bloom, clustered in such concentration that the atelier's ceiling fell out of view. Sunlight trickled between the five-petaled beauties and cast shuddering polygons of light on the ground.

Up ahead, Miss Lina wound between the trees, then disappeared from view. The Caregiver, meanwhile, strolled at a leisurely pace far behind me, hand outstretched to caress the trees she'd planted for the old woman. Because the trees grew so close together, there was no way to tell when the pink bounty of one ended and when another began. A cloud of imperceptible bounds seemed to be hovering just over my head. But sometimes the sun hit just right and made the blossoms flare into a passionate hue of violet. In those moments, they acquired the carbuncled solidity of flesh, and I felt like a cell pulsating through a giant lung.

I came upon Miss Lina standing under a tree. I could see her only from the back, her shoulders lurching from the savage force of her tears. I thought she was alone, but two pale shapes began to creep around her waist. They were hands, slowly reaching for each other, then clasping at the small of her back. Someone was rising to their feet, their black hair cresting over the old woman's head.

"I'm sorry it took me so long to find you," Miss Lina said. "You wouldn't believe all the people and places I've had to encounter on my way here. As soon as I lost you, my life did its utmost to distract me from finding you again. People needed me here, other people needed me there . . . But how did you manage all by yourself? Let me see. My goodness, you've gotten so big. Now you'll have to carry me around. And your face— what a mesmerizing surface . . . You'll forgive me, won't you?"

"There's nothing to forgive. I would have waited for you my entire life."

My heart shot forward. The second voice had the ringing purity of a bell. It wasn't a human voice, but the airy apotheosis from which all other voices were gristly deviations.

The boy rested his chin on Miss Lina's shoulder. He looked just like Moon. He wore nothing more than white linen trousers and a white T-shirt, as if to offer himself up for controlled observation. Indeed, the details I'd always loved were there: the plush lips, the wide cheeks, the slat-like eyes. But I couldn't advance from thinking he looked like Moon to thinking he was Moon. In fact, his resemblance possibly proved he wasn't Moon. Similarity precluded equivalence: if the boy were Moon, I'd never say he looked like Moon, just like I'd never say that I looked like myself.

There was a twig poised under my foot; I applied pressure to see what would happen. The boy turned his head at the sound. For the first time in our lives, Moon was looking at me. I'd always thought that as soon as he was within reach, I would have no choice but to announce that I loved him. But I did not run for him, I did not say a word. Now that we were in a room together, I found that I didn't know how to feel love for him with visceral conviction, having experienced this love so much across distance, through yearning. I was no less certain of my feelings, but they seemed to sit on a shelf higher than the hands of my immediate experience could reach.

He looked away, expression unaltered, as if my presence were no more to be expected than one of the trees. With a tremor, I wondered if he'd seen me at all. But there was no doubt that if I took three loping steps, I, too, could hold him in my arms. A gust of wind broke through the atelier, sending thousands of blossoms into susurrous abrasion. Swathed in that sound, which seemed to live through and beyond this forest to span ecosystems I'd never experienced before, I found it hard to believe we were in the same room.

"Let me take another look," Miss Lina said. "Can it be? I've missed you so much that I can scarcely believe I've found you."

She patted his face all over, as if trying to find a tumor of authenticity underneath.

"Don't doubt yourself," Moon said. "I'm exactly who you think I am. I don't know how to be anyone else."

I LAY IN bed in the guest room, staring at the richly embossed ceiling, where cherubs were nuzzling thick tangles of grapes. It was so hot that I'd stripped down to just my underwear.

Earlier that evening, instead of heading for dinner, I'd idled in my room before the mirror, alternately intoxicated and horrified by the fact that Moon had seen my face, its raw details, the patent emotion of my eyes. When I finally made it downstairs, I could hear muffled voices through the door to the dining room—everyone was already inside. But I couldn't bring myself to enter. The idea of chirping "Hello, nice to meet you" to Moon over a meal made my stomach turn. And what would we talk about? I couldn't ask like some flappy-mouthed reporter why he'd retired. What I needed were sinuous lines of poetry charged with enigmatic meaning—but not so obscure that he would be forced to request a clarification. I refused to make Moon complicit in the bungling of my own drama. Roundly defeated, I'd slunk away and returned to my room.

Now I lay on my back, immobilized by remorse, staggered by my own stupidity.

I was finally on the cusp of sleep when the footsteps began. I jerked awake. Someone was walking slowly in a straight line overhead, the floor creaking with every step. I knew it was Moon. The quiet resolve, the sensual lassitude—it had to be him. The noise weakened as he strayed beyond the demarcations of my room. But then he returned. He came to a sudden stop about a meter to my right—then resumed his steps, crossing over to the opposite side. Was he staying in the attic? If so, his room seemed to be twice the size of mine. My chamber, fit for a child, was encompassed by his from above.

I held my breath and lay still, awakening to a force of passion I hadn't felt since my arrival.

He moved back and forth over my room, his pauses occurring more and more in my proximity. My ceiling, his floor—this panel of wood had been set in place so that we wouldn't crash into each other with the violence of desire. The world, with its stolid rules concerning the final balance of all matter, would never let the amassment of our energy go unchecked. Would we always have to be so apart? Yet we gave each other meaning. I was his hell, he my heaven. We were indispensable to each other in our separation. I understood this with new clarity now that we were together in this house, closer than we'd ever been before. Perhaps this panel of wood, precisely for dividing us, was the only way to sustain the strength of our connection. But what would happen if we destroyed it for good?

Moon stopped directly overhead. There was a muffled noise, like the rubbing of two dishcloths against each other.

Was he lying down on the ground, to bring the entire length of his body closer to mine?

I slipped off my underwear. I gazed past my chin at my body. Anything could happen to it—a knife could come flying out of the darkness, the ceiling could fall without warning. I ran my hands all over my stomach with admiration and pity both. My hands—where should my hands go next? I clawed at my upper arms as though I were a stranger to entreat. I was not enough for myself, my body was not enough, yet I needed it, I couldn't think or feel anything limitless without it. I curled up onto my side in rapid contraction and stuck my knuckles into my mouth to stifle a cry that didn't erupt out of my throat so much as it drifted down from Moon's room to overtake and instrumentalize me.

10. Kinship

I AWOKE DESPONDENT AS USUAL, faced with the formidable task of finding Moon somewhere in the world. But as the haze of sleep lifted, the task narrowed into the far more achievable one of finding Moon somewhere around the Sanctuary. For a few minutes, I was too disoriented to move out of bed.

Suddenly unable to bear the idea of him roaming the house without me, I got up and dressed in a hurry—or perhaps he was still asleep. Buoyed by this thought, I bounded down the stairs with a feeling of pristine potential, an advantage measurable in seconds.

But Moon wasn't in the dining room. I did, however, finally catch a glimpse of Mister Suguk. He was a trim man with an aquiline profile and a pair of unusually large hands folded in his lap. He seemed to be keeping them at bay from the world, afraid they might accomplish more than he personally intended. His food was going cold. When Miss Lina tugged at his sleeve, he turned to her with slow recognition, like she was hailing from a misty distance.

"Do you know where my younger brother is?" she asked.

"You worry too much," Mister Suguk said serenely. "I'm sure he's closer than you think."

Farther down the table, the Caregiver was helping Mister Goun eat, but he kept pushing food back out of his mouth to ask for the time. I noticed this was dampening the mood of the normally unflappable woman. Still, she answered him without fail, and always down to the second.

"How can I eat?" Miss Lina began to moan. "How can I possibly eat?"

"I ask myself that, too," the Caregiver said, nodding seriously. "Still, I would love for all of you to go on living. I encourage it very much. Not because it's any fun. We know better than most how stunning the despair can be, perfect in its meaninglessness like the structure of an ice crystal. But we must see our miserable experiences through to the end."

I prowled the rest of the house in search of Moon. Strangely, I couldn't find stairs that would lead up to the attic. Then I remembered the stone turret. I went outside, where I fell into powerful disorientation at the sight of the sun blazing psychotically over the lake, whose plasticine surface accelerated in all directions for kilometers—it was hard to believe that any of this had been happening while I'd been tucked away in the Sanctuary. I walked around the house until I found the turret, internalizing its position. But when I went back inside and tried to move in its direction, I kept ending up in the kitchen. The Sanctuary was manifestly against me: Cook, it said, forget love.

In Miss Lina's atelier, I found the cherry blossoms in rapid and systematic decay. Brown clumps plummeted all around me with an undignified squelch. The ground, heaped with these moist deaths, steamed in the sun. So ruthless was the deterioration that I felt as though the atelier wasn't progressing through a season of change but moving in reverse, setting its dials back to zero. Moon, as it turned out, was not waiting for me at the tree.

But then there were footsteps in the distance.

I positioned myself with all the charm and elegance I could muster, wanting to leave Moon no doubt in his mind that he should pick me up and carry me away. But it was Miss Lina who found me. Before I could apologize, she took me into her arms and said everything I'd heard her say to Moon the previous day. And I responded with everything I'd heard Moon say. After all, it was easier for Miss Lina to believe I was her brother than it was for me to believe she was Moon. When she pulled away to examine my face, it seemed to be gratification, not incredulity, that widened her eyes. I must have looked just as she remembered.

. . .

WHEREVER I WENT, I worried that Moon was now in the place I'd left behind. So I headed back to the dining room. There, I found Mister Suguk eating with newfound gusto. A young woman I'd never seen before had taken Miss Lina's place at his side. I found the stranger's outfit wholly illegible: a fast-fashion T-shirt evoking the pleasures of nightlife, khaki cargo pants, and black rubber safety shoes. The intense disorder of her look brought it all to nothing; I couldn't see her as wearing anything in particular.

The old man appeared to be admonishing the girl:

"Stay here with me. With the further training of your already excellent mind, you will rise quickly to the top of your class. In you I see the seeds of an astonishing thinker, a blazing torch for those who have lost their way."

"There's no hope for me, Teacher," the girl said. "I'm mediocre just like everyone else. Whenever I'm faced with a decision, it's inevitably between two lukewarm options. So I fall into bed from exhaustion and proceed to have no dreams."

"Your soul must rise above the masses."

"My soul has to be back at work tonight. My soul needs money. And a bigger apartment."

I sat opposite the pair, mesmerized by the girl. Her small strong body, I felt, belonged to a sailor—arms that pulled at ropes, a stance that never lost its balance. Her black hair was gathered into a thick braid that snaked around the side of her neck and down to her stomach. Her skin had the translucence of an insect's wings, but there was nothing innocent about its purity. Instead, it possessed the quiet heroism of having passed defiantly through life without protection, only to emerge unscathed. Amidst this opalescence hovered her dark eyes.

"What do you do for work?" I asked, unable to help my curiosity.

"I work at a seafood restaurant," she said. "I'm usually way in the back, knifing open a dead skate with one hand and holding my nose with the other. I've been banned from the front of the house. Too many customers complained that I looked like I was about to throw up while I served their food."

"You were bad for business," I said approvingly.

"I'm just sensitive to the smell. I take a single whiff and know the skate stood no chance. I should get used to it, though. It's what I'll smell like soon enough."

"What do you mean?" I objected. "You're still so young. Nothing has been decided yet."

"I've been in and out of a juvenile detention center for years," she said with an amused smile. "The logical result of my contact with the world seems to be: me getting sent back to the center. Anyway, let's see. I've been out for a few months now."

I was startled to find the Caregiver watching this young guest with naked pity. I tried to imagine what kind of crimes the girl might have committed—arson, perhaps. I sensed she had the necessary self-awareness, a certain lack of narcissism, that would allow her to relinquish total authorship of her violence; she wouldn't mind letting a fire spread out of her control.

"I haven't seen you before," she said. "Whose kin might you be?"

"No one's. I'm here to see Moon."

"Moon," she said, like she was jogging her memory. "Are you an old friend of his?"

"Not exactly. We met for the first time yesterday. But I've wanted to meet him for a long time."

Her eyes narrowed.

"You're a fan," she said flatly.

"Not exactly . . ."

"Is there anything you're exact at being?" she said. "Watch out. You might hurt Moon's feelings with that kind of evasion. I like to tell Moon straight to his face that I'm the opposite of his fan. But he shouldn't take it personally. I'm incapable of putting anyone on a pedestal. I see the worst in people."

Whenever the girl blinked, her eyes ended up somewhere new on Mister Suguk's body; I never caught them moving. The old man was gulping down a glass of water and palpably blooming with strength. When he drew a napkin over his drooping mouth, he was instantly transformed into an elegantly aged movie star.

"You should've seen my father back in the day," the girl said. "I'm not embarrassed to say that he was taken seriously as a sexual candidate wherever he went."

"So he isn't your teacher," I said.

"He used to be. And a very good one. I think he always wanted to be my teacher more than he wanted to be my father. Well, his dream came true. He must've been onto something, because our relationship has never been better."

She laid a hand on the back of her father's head.

"Teacher," she said. "Let's go."

Mister Goun's head jerked up.

"Where?" he called out from the end of the table. "Where are you going?"

"We will travel the world," Mister Suguk said, rising from his seat with energy.

"I also want to travel the world," Mister Goun said.

"I'm sorry, my friend," Mister Suguk said. "But you are too broken."

Mister Goun leaned his head back and shut his eyes.

"I'm not broken," he said. "I'm just very tired."

WE FOUND MOON alone in Mister Suguk's atelier. Dressed in a dark blue uniform for schoolboys, he was standing before a chalkboard, pulling down a map. I was surprised by how well he fit into the musty charm of the classroom, which was crowded with kinking rows of wooden desks. The girl swept past Moon without saying hello and seated herself in the last row, where she crossed her arms with a pert sigh, refusing to meet his eyes. I struggled to guess what he could have possibly done to exasperate her so. Mister Suguk, however, was pleased to see the boy.

"Student Council President," the old man said, "I trust you have all our affairs in order—the treasury, the attendance sheet, the list of prizes that my students will win someday."

Moon responded with a deep bow. When Mister Suguk continued on to his desk in the corner of the room, I was left to linger alone by the door. I wondered if I should step forward and introduce myself as a new foreign exchange student. But Moon, sensing my unease, turned to me with a warm smile. Inordinately prepared to treasure whatever he was about to say, I swept every thought off the table of my brain.

"Hello, Miss Oseol," he said.

I stopped breathing. Meeting as we were for the second time, I was now someone he recognized, which meant that he'd possibly looked forward to seeing me. I wanted to tell him my real name so that I could hear him say it. But the girl called out from the back of the room before I could open my mouth.

"This lady followed us all the way from the dining room," she said. "I didn't have the heart to tell her to go away. I could smell it, that oily dissatisfaction with her own life—"

"Maehwa," Moon said. "Stop it."

"I like it so much when you give me commands," Maehwa said, shutting her eyes. "I don't want to think for myself anymore."

I blinked in shock. They were using the informal register. Even their intonation had changed—quicker, mercurial. It was a manner of speaking I'd observed among high schoolers on the subway in Seoul, huddled together with the feverish secrecy of a coven.

"If you would prefer me to leave," I blurted, "just say so."

I cringed. I was resorting to clichés in my state of confusion.

"No, stay," Maehwa said. "I'm curious to know how it feels to be someone like you. To think you really know someone when you don't know them at all."

"But I feel like I've known Moon my whole life—"

"I could almost find that beautiful," she said dryly. "You know, my father and I had all the time in the world to get to know each other. Even so, nothing but blood connected us for years. A lot had to happen before we could know each other. I had to lose my name; I had to become someone else entirely. So for you to say that you know Moon—well, that's frankly outrageous to me."

At that moment, Mister Suguk clapped for everyone's attention. Moon sat down in the first row, but I headed for the back of the room and cowered by the wall, consumed by misery. What was this "a lot" that brought two people together, if not blood, nor shared experience across time? To my disturbance, Maehwa seemed to be suggesting that whatever it was, she'd experienced this "a lot" not only with her father but with Moon as well.

The lesson began. Mister Suguk pointed at the map hanging over the chalkboard. It was a cartographical monstrosity: he'd sliced a world atlas into dozens of vertical strips and arranged them into a new order. The result was a spastic composite of blue and green. I could identify no country, no ocean. Gone were the patiently winding curves of a bay, artless blocks of land. Nothing sprawled. Sometimes a few slivers of green pieced themselves together across the strips with jerky fortitude, but they were inevitably cut short by blue.

"When one lives deeply, the world looks like this," Mister Suguk said. "What good is geography if it prioritizes the immediacy of physical experience at the expense of everything else? Your pen pals are proof that you are not just here. You are also where they are. And they, in turn, are where you are. Student Council President, I would like for you to read first today."

Moon stood up at his desk with an abused-looking piece of paper, its edge frayed from having been roughly torn out of a notebook. He had to lay it flat on his desk and smooth it out before he could begin.

"Dear Moon," he read aloud, "I am sending you a boomerang. Don't ask me where in Australia I live. I don't remember the name of my town. Work has been terribly busy. How I wish the restaurant would shut down! There are so many other things that could take its place: horse stable, boxing gym, observation tower. Pick your favorite. I will make sure your choice exists by the time you visit. In return, you can help me complete my remaining hours of community service at the youth center. The orphans will like you so much better than me. You asked if Australians eat or dance or think or breathe in any special way. Nothing comes to mind, I'm afraid! Except the boomerang. You better not send it back. In this particular case, I do not want the boomerang to work . . ."

Moon read to the end with utmost seriousness, sometimes pausing after a line that struck me as no more significant than the lines preceding. It was a strange letter, intimate and characterless at once. Personal details were so few as to be conspicuous. I glanced over at Maehwa—she was examining her nails with a smile.

"And the boomerang?" Mister Suguk said. "Where is it?"

"Oh," Moon said, looking around as though he'd misplaced the gift. "It's gone . . ."

"You're in luck," Mister Suguk said sternly. "I would've snapped it in half over my knee. What do I always say? No souvenirs. No objects should be flying in the air between you and your correspondent."

Now it was Maehwa's turn. She rose to her feet with a crisp sheet of paper densely packed with black script, front and back. I recognized the handwriting immediately.

THIS WAS WHAT Moon had written Maehwa:

"To my sister of the heart—no, don't tell me your name. We never need to be introduced. One day we will meet, and if I am so sure of it, then why not go ahead and assume that we already have. I take the future, and I implant it into the arm of the now. No, don't send me your portrait either. Stay ghostly. Then, you are everywhere . . .

"You ask for news. I have a swimming teacher. I'm not engaged to her. It's not like that; it never is. The story is always one of disjuncture, not of a joyful coming together! Like my body and water. Swimming does not come naturally to me. I have been compelled to walk. I can't make a single appointment that isn't immediately canceled, so I follow around strangers who appear fashionably busy, and I make my shadow interlock with theirs in painless combat. My swimming teacher was no exception. I knew only the back of her head for a long time. I was in the midst of following her one day when she spun around on her heels and said she consented to being my teacher. I hadn't even asked. I didn't need to. She'd known from the weariness of my footsteps that I'd grown sick of my achievements on land.

"I want you to have a clear picture of my swimming teacher. She's not a pretty woman. She has a long crooked spine, but it is marvelous at helping her wind through the water like an eel. One of her eyes is much larger than the other. But she sees less out of that eye. The parts of her that are supposed to match never do. When she puts her hands on her lover in the dark, he screams out in fright, believing there to be a third person in the room. Only her two front teeth, the big ones, are identical. They are white like headstones. She smiles a cemetery at her loved ones, of which there are few. As you might imagine, she prefers the murky lethargy of life underwater. She's rather good-humored for someone who can't get anything right on land. She almost dies from laughter as she tells me that she's running out of time, that it's painful to be so useless at her own tremendous existence, to be the worst example of herself.

"Our first swimming lesson was the last. She took me to the biggest lake in the region. It was past midnight. She stood on the shore with a samovar chugging at her feet and pointed at the lake. 'Get in there,' she barked. She hadn't told me anything about how I should move my arms or legs. But I'd always promised her my unabiding obedience. So I waded into the lake. When I was up to my shoulders, I turned around and awaited further instructions. 'And?!' my teacher cried out from shore. I threw myself backward. I opened my eyes—the water was black like ink under the moonless sky. I waited to come upon the ability to swim. But I could feel myself starting to sink. How strange, I thought, to have been capable of dying all this time. So then I waited to touch ground and molder there. But this moment, too, would not come. With horror, I realized that I was in the midst of absolute suspension, surrounded by water on all sides. The loneliness was so excruciating that it triggered my first moment of pain. I clawed at the water over my head, wanting something, anything at all, to change.

"Then it happened. My body hit upon its perfect choreography of existence. I had never even known to consider the possibility of such a movement, yet at that moment I was certain I'd been waiting for it my entire life. The movement was not mine. I did not create it; it used me to birth itself. It happened to me with the force of violation. I was being given a second chance at life, to rush upon its terrain with the fresh knowledge that there existed an arrangement of my body in space wherein every one of my cells, bursting with health, was conscripted to truth—how could that not change everything, even the sight of a face I despised? And yet the price I would have to pay was the bludgeoning fact that I could never recreate this movement on land, in the midst of life.

"I was not swimming. My teacher, I realized, did not teach swimming. Even now, I cannot say what it is my teacher teaches. I haven't had a chance to ask her. When I crawled back to shore, she was gone . . ."

After Maehwa was done reading, she continued gazing down at the letter, transfixed by the black script as though it were an optical illusion. Mister Suguk's eyes were closed; I wondered if he was asleep. Moon hung his head, having endured every word like a small punishment.

My hands were shaking uncontrollably. So Moon had been fantasizing about it, too—the dance that defied description, the move of my Moon dreams. After writing about it for months, carving out miles upon miles of my tunnel of imagination, I'd succeeded at making a break into his, creating a flow of secret knowledge between us. No one knew him like I did. This was no collaboration; this was collusion.

But it was impossible to extricate my joy from the wet strands of my suffering. Moon had expressed, in concise poetry, what bound us together—but he saw me no less as a perfect stranger. The letter was there, consummate, the indisputable manifesto of our shared fantasy—and yet it wasn't for me. In fact, an entirely different world would have to be built from scratch for Moon to write me such a letter. The irony was cruel. The proof of our connection sat deep inside his letter as if inside a glass box: nothing obscured my view of it, but I could not touch it, I could not claim it as my own.

I NEEDED SOMEONE to talk to. But the Caregiver had little attention to spare. She and Mister Goun were still in the dining room, though she was now helping him sort through a collection of family photographs, sprawled across the table in disorder. Noticing me at the door, she waved me over and explained that she'd given Mister Goun a photo album to fill with his favorite memories. There were also scissors, should he wish to "expunge" from his records anyone who'd hurt him beyond the possibility of forgiveness.

The old man had a surprisingly rigorous system. He would set two pictures against each other and contemplate them for a long time, whereupon he took one and flung it to the ground with theatrical distaste. Then a new round of deliberations would ensue. The floor around him was littered with photographs, while only a handful remained on the table, fewer than would fill the album to completion.

I observed the two pictures currently in competition. In the first, Mister Goun could be seen standing in a shoe factory with a giant banner bearing Chinese characters. There was nothing artisanal about the environs; I supposed he'd had to make certain concessions in his career. In the second, a young woman had her arms laced around Mister Goun as they stood under a trellis hanging with gourds. I recognized, to my shock, the Caregiver. She towered over Mister Goun in black heels. He was red in the face and portly. The two of them composed a single insouciant team and gave the impression of having deigned to step out of their dank lair of lovemaking for a few minutes.

The Caregiver caught the expression on my face.

"Don't be sad for me," she said. "I'm like a buried trauma. He might have forgotten me, but he'll never exorcize me. He loves me more than he knows—"

In one swift move, Mister Goun sent the second picture flying to the floor. The Caregiver leaned over to rescue it, then set it back on the table, ostensibly returning it for Mister Goun's consideration.

Here we were, I thought gloomily, the Caregiver and I, indefatigably following our distracted objects of affection around the house . . . All of a sudden, the frustration that had gathered in my heart since my arrival poured out in one epiphanic rush, and what took its place was radiant hope. Perhaps Moon, like Mister Goun, no longer remembered the person he loved most in the world. If this person was me, then perhaps, unable to bear the pain of his amnesia, I'd settled for a place among the faceless horde that adored Moon. Might this be why I'd always chafed at calling myself a fan? If so, the true source of my pain wasn't that Moon would never get to know me, but that he'd forgotten he already did. I simply had to remind him. But how? How might I remind him of a past that even I, for all my conviction, couldn't articulate?

Mister Goun dispatched another victim to the floor. In the picture, he was standing in a parking lot so vast that it extended beyond the frame. The parking lot must have served a venue visited by thousands of people at once, like a soccer arena or a megachurch. But there wasn't a single car in view. Mister Goun had his back to the camera but his face turned over his shoulder, hips twisting into decision—either to come back, or to go away forever.

11. The Repairman

AFTER THE CONCERT, Y/N BECOMES quiet and unexcitable. Her new hobby is taking apart old clocks. She finds them at antique markets all over Seoul. She is strict about bringing them home only one at a time; once, she'd made the mistake of bringing two, and the subtle discrepancy between their ticking had nearly driven her mad.

When she gets home, she walks around her apartment with the clock, cradling it in her hands like a small bomb. At her desk, she painstakingly dismantles it as she squints through a loupe. She arranges its tiny metal components in neat rows across her desk. Y/N loves the moment when, upon the decisive extraction of a tooth-like bit, the clock stops ticking. A supernatural silence falls around her. When she sees her hands lying still upon her desk, she can almost believe that they belong to a photograph—that she has slipped out of time. She can't imagine having a goal ever again.

Days pass without food or sleep. Y/N is now lying on the floor, surrounded by hundreds of disemboweled clocks. The room is dark; it must be evening. All of a sudden, the door opens, and someone steps into the apartment. It's a man carrying a toolbox. Y/N is too weak to do anything but watch as the man, without a word, steps over her body and proceeds to reassemble one clock after another. The room slowly fills with ticking of all kinds. The noise is growing torrential. The ticking is so multiple, so motley—dozens of cuckoo clocks among them—that it creates a single wash of noise.

Time, of a sort, passes. The repairman leaves as silently as he came. Y/N notices only when it's too late.

Her heart is starting to come alive amidst the cacophony of unsynced time. The repairman has restored not the linear march of a single human life but a roaring cascade that is eternity itself, so encompassing that when she relaxes her vigilance, she doesn't hear anything at all. The last time she felt this way was when she witnessed, between these same walls, Moon performing the dance move that defied description. In that moment, too, she glimpsed a sliver of eternity, a leakage from the mellifluous darkness encasing the visible world. Among the resuscitated clocks, she dreams of sending herself away, like a dove released, to that other realm. There she would be caught in the amber of her existence. She would never age again; she would forget her birthday.

Y/N is finally strong enough to stand up. As she looks around the room, she realizes that her favorite clock is missing: a pocket watch that opens and shuts like a clam, as if to suggest there are moments when one should not know the time. The repairman has taken it with him. In the absence of its singular ticking, four clicks to a second, she hears herself being called.

She packs a suitcase and leaves the apartment, her ears cocked for the pocket watch. She seeks quiet places, like chapels and landfills. Whenever a sparrow chitters neurotically in her proximity, she stamps a foot to make it fly away. She walks and walks, ending up in a city of staggering proportions, but, with the repairman nowhere to be seen, she keeps walking, and this city slowly becomes another city, which becomes yet another city, until Y/N, too exhausted to take another step, falls onto her back on the sidewalk. Her suitcase collapses next to her like an obliging sidekick. Y/N's view of the blue sky is obliterated by brand-new apartment towers that have yet to be occupied . . .

I put down my pen. I didn't know what should come next.

It seemed likely that Y/N would move from city to city in perpetuity. She would never find the repairman, yet she would never lose the conviction that he existed somewhere in the world to be found. And this conviction alone would mean everything. But there was also the chance, however slight, that as she lay there, at the feet of those apartment buildings, a single window would suddenly light up in one of their concrete flanks. Y/N would take the elevator high into the atmosphere and find the repairman waiting in an apartment furnished with nothing but a bed they must share. The rest of the building, all thirty floors, would be empty.

I was struck by insight: it was imperative that Moon read my story. For here, in this notebook, was our lost history. Here, in these scenes, was the symbolic shadowplay of all that had already transpired between us. But the events to come after— they defied my imagination. What I did know was that in this unimaginable future, we would be together at last, away from the world, freed from its detrimental gravity. We would encounter each other in infinitude. We would shuck off our bodies and surge toward each other as souls. Together in our renunciation of reality, we would achieve what no fan and his star had ever achieved before: mutual universality, perfect love.

I TRIED THE kitchen. To my surprise, Moon was there, standing at the counter, back turned to me, cracking an egg into a glass bowl. I considered calling for him, but I couldn't bear the sterility of using his name in such a functional way. In the hundreds of times I'd said his name before, not once had I said it to him directly, much less to crudely demand his attention. The syllable had always fit my mouth like a wistful sigh.

"What are you making?" I asked.

He turned around with a ready smile.

"Nothing," he said. "I just wanted to know what cooking feels like."

The kitchen table had two chairs positioned on perpendicular sides, as if a couple who preferred the proximity of their bodies to a direct view of each other's faces had just finished a meal. Moon and I sat down.

"How can I help you, Miss Oseol?" he asked.

I laid my notebook on the table, turned the cover, and pushed it toward him.

"I would like for you to read something I wrote."

"But it's in English," he said, peering down at the first page.

"You don't need to understand every word. What's important is to grasp the general idea. Take your time, I can wait."

To my pleasure, he picked up the notebook and began to read aloud. I relished the gaminess of his accent; it sounded impossible to fix. He paused when he came across the word Y/N. He tried pronouncing it as "yin," but immediately reconsidered, settling instead on "why en." Each time he uttered the abbreviation, I increasingly understood myself in the sound—the breathy insubstantiality of "why," which was pulled down the throat by the density of "en." He seemed to be asking "why" of my existence, "why" I was what I was.

He turned a page and kept reading. But when Moon the character appeared at the bus stop, he broke off mid-sentence.

"You wrote a story about me," he said.

"Yes," I said. "Now please keep reading."

But he flipped back to the first page and started over. This time, he read under his breath with impatience. Whereas earlier, he'd read aloud out of an instinctive desire to please, now he was reading to understand. On occasion, he spoke up to ask what a word meant. He'd assumed that Y/N stood for "Yes/ No," believing the slash to signify the protagonist's fragmented sense of self. When I clarified that it stood for "Your Name," he grew only more confused.

"If I'm supposed to replace Y/N with my own name, then is this a story about me interacting with myself?" he asked. "And what about me could possibly remind you of a philosopher? I don't know anything about philosophy."

Moon was now several pages into the story. Whenever his namesake appeared, his eyes flashed with pleasure and suspicion: "Who's more realistic—me or him?" he asked. "Who leads the stranger life?" He kept waiting for the story to "get me right," as if this would prove that he'd conveyed a neat package of selfhood to the public. Then he would be sure that who he was on the outside corroborated who he was on the inside. But whenever the story achieved an accurate depiction, he seemed to resent the assumption that he could ever be known. In sum, the character could do nothing right.

He reached the scene where Y/N bikes down a Berlin street naked, throws herself off, and skids down the asphalt. She uses the pus from her lacerated body to fry up the most delicious meals of Moon's life. It is an early courtship maneuver.

Moon groaned in disgust. "Don't take it so personally," I said. But whether it was what Y/N did or what Moon ate that he took personally, I wasn't sure.

Moon stopped reading after that. He tapped his fingers on the notebook, then slid it back to me.

"Seems like an interesting story," he said, as if he'd been hearing about it from someone else.

"You barely made it past the first chapter," I said. "Please read until the end. There's so much I have to tell you. But talking is no good; my words emerge too much in a row. This story is my way of saying everything at once. When it sinks in, you'll realize that I know you better than anyone else does and that I love you with a pure heart."

Moon was examining me carefully.

"I still can't tell where your accent is from," he said slowly. "It makes you sound lighthearted, like you're joking. But what you say is never funny. The strange formality of your tone . . . Yes, I know what it is: you speak Korean like a newscaster from an elapsed decade. Yet you mangle the pronunciation of the simplest words. Did someone send you? A company, a government? No, I can't imagine any group dispatching you as their representative. I can't even imagine you being someone's daughter. The first time I saw you, I thought—what an oddly unclear person . . . like a window covered in dust . . ."

"I'm not a stranger. You know me. All of your videos, pictures, messages—they were for me. Don't make that face, it's true. You couldn't have known it at the time, since you didn't know who I was, but you didn't need to. Our connection preceded us. I have spent my entire life training myself to feel the feelings I have for you. My perception has been perfectly notched to match the gear of your personality."

"Don't think I haven't heard this all before," he said.

"That can't be true," I said, vexed. "No one thinks like I do. Look. Five months ago I was in Germany watching videos of you. Now I'm here. But I feel farther away from you than ever. I don't miss you because I love you. I love you because I miss you. I used to love the emptiness of my computer screen just for having once contained you."

Moon's face showed neither confusion nor understanding.

"Germany," he repeated.

"It doesn't matter. Where I come from doesn't matter. I use all of me to know you. Knowing you is the most serious task of my life. I love the world I hate simply because you live in it. Watching you dance brings tears to my eyes. But I never full-on cry. It's more like the tears are extending the boundaries of my eyeballs, making me see differently. Some would say 'badly,' but I don't agree with them at all. You are not an object to me. You are not a toy. It's the opposite. You are far too real to me. I've looked at you so much. It's frightening, actually, how I will never not know what you look like. I usually feel nothing when I kiss a person, but the next day, I obsess over the kiss. I feel it even more intensely than when the kiss was actually happening. I love you because you are this paradox. You are so there in your missing. I want to live as you dance. You move and move and move—and you don't go anywhere at all. I want . . ."

The sound of my own voice was starting to make me sick. Why wasn't I capable of the seriousness of simplicity? Or perhaps I hadn't said enough. Perhaps communication was a stamina sport. I went on:

"I need more time. I need at least a year with you. Let's go somewhere together. Where do you have the fewest fans? Mallorca? Be around me a lot. You'll realize what I'm like. We need proper space and time. So that we can simply be. There should be no pressure to get to know each other. That's how much faith I have in our connection. Everything would come about organically . . . I wish we'd met through mutual friends. I wish our families had gone to the same church. Don't you see how hopeless my situation is? It's not my fault. I could come to know you only in this strange way. But you can make the difference. You can give me hope."

Moon hardened his face.

"And why would I do that?" he said.

"I know I've done nothing to earn your trust. But trust me anyway. Take the risk. Bring the match to the gas. Just imagine what could happen. Aren't you curious? Even a little bit?"

"Let's say I agree to everything you propose," he said. "Then what? I've been wondering about you, Miss Oseol. I've been asking myself: Doesn't she know by now that it was a mistake to come all the way here? Shouldn't she be with her friends, her family? Why doesn't she go home? Of all the places in the world—why would you want to be here? You won't find anything at my side. Our futures can never align."

"But our presents have aligned," I said. "So why can't our futures? Especially if I invest all of my energy into making sure it does. You see for yourself that I got here on my own. So imagine all that could happen if you played your part. Say yes."

"Look," he said gently. "I don't know what you've been through. I don't know how to help you. Please understand, I'm just one person. But here's what I can do. Make a specific request of me. I can give you something I own, I can take a picture with you . . . If it's something I can manage, I promise I'll do it. Then you won't leave the Sanctuary feeling this was all for nothing."

I might as well have been speaking with a well-meaning relative. Here Moon was, setting before me ideas of indisputable rationality, like utensils arranged in order, polished and practical, when he was supposed to be coaxing my imagination into its deepest contortions.

"Dance for me," I said.

"No," he said. "It's not time yet."

"Haven't you had enough rest by now?" I said in frustration. "Don't you miss it? How can you stand to be so far away from your art?"

"I do miss it," he said ruefully. "But some things are beyond my control. I only have myself to blame. I would always test my limits. Whenever Sun kept time by clapping his hands, I would fit as many dance steps between two beats as were supposed to fit between four. I'd seen so many incredible videos of myself. Sometimes I would play them at double speed. If my image could move that fast, why couldn't my body? Sun got angry whenever I sped up my moves. 'Your heart won't be able to take it anymore,' he said, and that's exactly what happened. The doctors cut me open and stuck a tiny metal contraption inside my heart. It looks like a toy for cats."

My mind went numb with confusion.

"You can't dance anymore," I said.

"I didn't say that," Moon said. "I can feel it inside of me still. Deep inside I know how to dance. The moment prior to striking a move—I can inhabit it even now. But the moment lasts no more than an instant, and without the force of my body securing it from the other side, it dissipates. One day I'll be strong enough to bring it to completion."

I couldn't bear to hear him reassure himself. His days of consecration were over. I wasn't sure I would've come to the

Sanctuary had I known he could no longer dance. It appeared that my love had conditions after all. Nothing brought love down to earth more than conditions, and nothing hurt my pride more than my love brought down to earth. The fact that I could threaten Moon with the withdrawal of my love didn't make me feel powerful. It made me feel intensely weak and empty.

"It's an illusion," I said dully. "You'll never dance again."

Moon opened and shut his mouth without making a sound, then got out of his chair and walked to the corner of the room, where he picked up the receiver of a black rotary phone.

"Who are you calling?" I asked, standing up.

"Maehwa."

I crossed the room, snatched the phone out of his hand, and pressed it to my ear. The plastic dimmed the noise of the world around me. There was nothing on the other end, not even a busy tone. Moon tore the receiver out of my hand and clutched it to his chest.

"It's too late," I said. "Maehwa doesn't know what I know. I know what you've lost, and so I know who you're supposed to be."

"What do you want from me?" he cried out.

There was suffering on his face. I'd seen this expression before, in the deepest throes of his dance. But what had once been beautiful, a lacquer stroke of elevation upon his features, only saddened me now. I suddenly missed Moon so much, I thought my chest would crack open from the velocity of the feeling.

"I wish you were Moon," I said.

He turned his head away from me, exposing his neck. There, a muscle pulsated just once, powerfully. I imagined that pulsation as a blue spirit traveling all the way down to his penis, which, unanchored, would jump in place, startled by the invasion. That line I'd always loved from the neck to the penis—this was the spirit's highway. Love for Moon pressed down upon my body all over again. I took hold of his shoulders and plunged into his neck. I dragged my lips across its skin, my hunger growing with every attempt to sate it. I didn't know where I was going. I didn't know where it was possible to go. His skin was a dead end.

Moon pushed me away. Adolescent cruelty glimmered in his eyes. He was breathing hard. His voice was soft but not at all gentle:

"Why didn't you say this was what you wanted? Were you ashamed to want the same thing as everyone else?"

"It's not what you think," I said, taking another step forward.

A weight knocked my head to the side. I blinked in pain, of all kinds. Through my tears, I could see Moon wielding the phone over his head, its cord quivering like the tail of a frightened animal.

THE FULL MOON was spilling its radioactive milk everywhere. I rolled onto my side and threw my arm across the bedsheet. Its inner crook appeared unusually tender tonight. I breathed as quietly as possible, afraid that I might miss the sound of Moon's footsteps overhead. But something else rose out of the silence. Something much faster and sharper than the dull thud of feet.

Infinitesimal crunches of metal. Four clicks per second.

I rose from bed and followed the noise out of my room. It guided me down the stairs and back to the kitchen. There were now two clicks per second. The closer I drew to the pocket watch, the more it slowed down. This was its way of telling me where to go.

I paced the kitchen, unsure of my next move. Then I saw that the door to the pantry was open. I entered to find its walls lined with glass jars of pickled vegetables turning slowly in their juices. To my surprise, the compartment grew larger with every step I took. I moved deeper and deeper inside, until the space swerved to the right, revealing a tightly winding staircase. When I reached the top, dizzy from all the circles I'd made, I found myself standing before a sliding wooden door, ajar by a centimeter. I peered through the crack.

Before me was a small room that lay directly under the Sanctuary's sloping roof. Maehwa was standing in a white dress that fell to her knees. Her hair was free from its braid. In the large awning window, the moon was the cross section of a boiled potato hanging over the lake, casting an abalone luster upon the water and the mountains rising in the distance. Maehwa reached her hand through the opening and gently pulled the window shut. The quiet of the room latched itself in.

She lowered herself onto the edge of a mat. Only then did I notice, amidst the tangle of white blankets, Moon asleep on his back. He had no shirt on, only a sheen of perspiration that accentuated the contours of his softly heaving chest.

The ticking was irregular, barely perceptible, all but dying now. At times, the pounding of blood in my ears obscured the noise entirely.

Moon's eyes were still shut in sleep when he began a fitful struggle to free himself from a sheet twisted around his waist. Once liberated, he threw his arms over his head, making his back arch and his ribs rise. And then I saw it, the part of him that I had always wondered about. Its sudden appearance shocked me nonetheless. Moon's arms and legs were flung out in the shape of a star in the stifling heat, but the penis was curled into itself. Its season was winter. There was something vague yet resolute about it, as if it had spent the night drinking and was now swooning in the depths of strange dreams, unafraid of what it had to confront in the secret world of itself.

Maehwa slid a hand across Moon's chest until her fingers curved around his side. She hooked herself there as if he were the edge of a cliff. She tilted up her head, alert to something in the air. Had she heard the ticking, too?

The penis began a steady expansion into itself, the tip unsheathing, its contours sharpening. What was once as soft as an eyelid was now as hard as a rock. As the penis rose straight into the air, it assumed the appearance of an ancient arrowhead. It cast a baleful gaze upon its surroundings as its master remained sunk in unconsciousness. But Moon's hand suddenly rose from the mat. Maehwa did not turn her head to look at it. I watched as the hand slowly came to a rest on the side of her face. She bent her neck to enter the caress more deeply.

"It's here, isn't it?" she said.

"Almost."

Moon's hand fell away from her face and landed upon her hand. He held it for a moment—merely held it—then moved it a few centimeters lower on his chest.

"There," he said, as if his heart were a distant shore.

12. Pure Future

UPON RETURNING FROM THE SANCTUARY, I considered buying a flight out of Seoul to depart that very evening. But I didn't know where I wanted the flight to take me. I was sick of traveling. What I wanted was someone or something to follow.

My tourist visa was set to expire at midnight. I had a four p.m. appointment at the immigration office to apply for a heritage visa, but on my way there, I made the impulsive decision to exit the subway station instead of boarding my transfer. On the crowded escalator up to the street, I had the sensation that all of us, squinting with confusion into the blast of sun, were being safely delivered out of a bomb shelter but feeling unhappy about the straightforward responsibilities that awaited us.

When O opened the door, I gave a sorry smile. This hurt my face because I hadn't smiled in a long time. Her cheeks were gaunt and sallow, and her hair was thrown up into a haphazard bun. But I noticed that her eyes were shining with unusual power. She turned them away, as if to spare me, and stepped aside to let me in.

The living room wasn't how I remembered it. The plasma screen had been replaced with a much larger model. It wasn't on, but it emanated an ugly impatience to be brought back to life, instead of receding quietly into the room. The couch had been pushed aside to make space for an electric massage bed, which suggested that O's mother now liked to watch the news by lying on the contraption with her head turned sharply to the side. There was a subwoofer speaker standing next to it. I imagined the woman pressing her hand against its shuddering mesh to feel upon her skin that which she could not hear.

O's mother appeared to be in her bedroom with the door closed. Meanwhile, the door to the veranda was open. Cicadas were lusting in multitudes. There must have been cicadas crying out at the Sanctuary as well, but strangely, I couldn't remember the last time I'd been conscious of the noise. O's apartment seemed to be the only place left on earth where my ears could recover their virginal astonishment. Since returning to Seoul, I'd been avoiding thinking about Moon, but now I recalled, with intense pain, how my body had traversed those two days in complete error.

All of a sudden, a female voice, at once strident and coquettish, resounded through the living room: "Hello. For your safety, for your children's safety, for the safety of the elderly, for your pets' safety, and for the safety of your indoor plants, please keep your windows shut between the hours of four and six p.m. Hello. For your safety, for your children's safety . . ." The woman sounded annoyed with her addressee for having gotten involved with so many things that could die. Once she'd repeated her injunction in full, there was a shrill beep, then a return to the swelling chorus outside.

"What was that?" I asked.

O gestured at the intercom on the wall.

"The building management has been playing that message all day," she said. "The number of cicadas has grown out of control this year. It's impossible to walk past the trees below. Cicadas everywhere. It's dangerous, pretty much like walking through a cloud of shrapnel. You must've come from the other side of the building. Anyway, a company will come and spray a special chemical on the trees."

"What's special about it?" I asked.

"First the cicada's legs fall off," O said. "Then its skin cracks open. The internal organs slide out intact. All fluids promptly evaporate. The massacre will be easy to clean up."

I glanced up at the clock. It was five minutes to four. I thought of my appointment at the immigration office. I liked pretending there was still a chance of obtaining a heritage visa. There wasn't. But anything felt possible in the few minutes between where I was and where I was supposed to be.

O stood on the threshold of the veranda, pausing to observe a cicada clinging to the wire screen. The insect buzzed with ferocity, as if issuing a personal threat against O. It flew away like a war helicopter, then dropped out of the air in seeming malfunction. More cicadas visited the balcony, always briefly and one at a time. It was as if a disagreement had broken out among the cicadas in the trees below, and now they were attempting to strike out on their own by rising high into the air, where, trapped between the colorless facade of one apartment tower and another, they lost their fortitude and plunged back into the disgruntled swarm.

It was now one minute to four. Outside, a machine could be heard whirring to gargantuan life. It was with seeming reluctance that O finally shut the veranda door.

We went to her bedroom. I sat on the edge of O's bed and looked around. The lights were off, but a bit of sun filtered through the room's only window. Her paintings were nowhere to be seen.

"It's strange to be back in Seoul," I said.

"Where were you?" she asked.

"Somewhere else."

O closed the door and reached high above the frame, unfurling a white bedsheet. She smoothed out the wrinkles but could do nothing about the doorknob bulging through the fabric. She joined me on the edge of the bed and set a projector machine on her lap.

"I was also somewhere else," she said.

"Is that so?" I said. "Strange that I didn't run into you."

"Somewhere else is very big," she said.

There was a new reserve about O. She didn't seem to belong to her own room anymore. I had the sense that she really had been somewhere else, perhaps more somewhere else than I had been. It even seemed possible that I hadn't been somewhere else at all. Before I could ask her anything about it, she clicked on the projector.

THE FILM BEGAN. O appeared on the bedsheet, playing the part of a painter. In all aspects of her life, this painter commits to nothing and believes in nothing. She lives in pursuit of visual noise, filling her canvas with anything but white. She has virtuosic technique, but sometimes it strikes her as meaningless for lack of a perfect subject. She has style without content, idiosyncrasy without a mission, personality without a point.

The painter has one friend, a writer, played by a Korean woman who looked nothing like me. This writer rambles on and on about her obsession with a man. The writer is the painter's exact foil: she possesses no technical capability, no style, no idiosyncrasy, having surrendered too much of herself to the perfect subject. When she is not talking about the man, she is writing about him. Her sprawling texts, composed in a trance, escape her own comprehension. Her beloved, who never shows up in the film, is a vortex into which her artistic potential has disappeared.

At one point, the writer says: "I conceive of the mind as a shirt. Every idea is a button or a hole. We pair up ideas, button to hole, so that the two parts of the shirt align and sit well upon the body. But I want my shirt to misalign so that it presses against the body in the wrong places. I want nothing to fit. The button entering the wrong hole—I worship this vector. This vector is the future. That's why I love him. He is that vector spun like thread into human. He is pure future. It's not him that I love. I love the story of him. That's why I don't know how to write well. What's the point of writing well when the story is already perfect? I channel his story. I add nothing to it. I keep the broth spare and intense."

I'd never said these words before. The writer spoke in English with a heavy Korean accent.

In another scene, the painter and the writer stand before the water fountain at Children's Grand Park. They are watching a water show coordinated to exuberant love songs blasting over the park's speakers. The writer walks ahead and stands among the children stamping in the puddles that surround the fountain. Upon the song's propulsive entrance into the chorus, she shoots a hand into the air, conjuring a thick lance of water from the center of the fountain. She makes repeated scooping motions with her hand, urging the smaller streams of water along the fountain's edge to reveal themselves, all down the perimeter. The water is her dance troupe, and she their conductor.

The children back away, perturbed by how this adult plays.

Of course, the writer has no actual influence over the fountain. But she displays such prophetic sensitivity to its exertions that the painter is capable, for as long as the song lasts, of believing that the strange world in which she lives is in her friend's hands. The painter feels safe, nestled in the folds of an elusive external logic that loves her.

In the final scene, the two women are in the painter's bedroom. The camera captures them through the doorway. A canvas lies on the floor. The painter gets onto her hands and knees to peer over the edge of the canvas as though it were a pond. The writer looks over her friend's shoulder. That's when the painting, and only the painting, fills the screen.

In a voiceover, the painter delivers a monologue. She says that her first strokes on the canvas were devoted to the back of the writer's left knee; never before had she begun a portrait somewhere other than the subject's face. Once she fully rendered both knees, she coaxed them into telling her about the person to whom they belonged. In ringing unison, they said that they'd never seen their owner's face. All they knew was that she was always speaking to someone named Moon. What this meant, they couldn't be sure. Maybe all of her friends had the same name, Moon. Maybe she was still in bed with her lover, Moon. Maybe she worshipped a god, Moon. Whoever he was, the knees knew that the writer's precarious sense of self would crumble without him. So they liked to imagine Moon as existing on her very body.

Hearing this, the painter had a stroke of inspiration.

"I'm sick of faces," she says. "It's time that we see the world from a different perspective. Why can't we start seeing from the backs of our knees? Why can't we see each other knee to knee, instead of face to face?"

I stood up and drew toward the bedsheet. The painting was a nude portrait of the back of my body. In it, my hair was black and buzzed short. I was looking over my left shoulder, but I had my neck twisted to such an abnormal extent that you could see my entire face. The folds in my neck were like the spiraling ridges of a screw; my head was lodging itself ever deeper into the slot between my shoulders. But that wasn't the strangest part. Moon's face seemed to have sprouted on my head and tectonically shifted my face to the left. His left cheek blended seamlessly into my right. Because the perspective privileged my face, his was visible only in part, but it likely existed in completion like mine. I was sharing my head with Moon. Neither of us were smiling.

Never before had such an image existed: Moon and I, together as one. In the painting, we merged with a perfection that other couples could only dream of. Our adjacent cheeks fused into one—this was more sexual than sex. I listened from the left ear, he from the right; we were spies on each other's behalf. The world aggressed us as one unit; we no longer experienced anything alone. When one of us laughed, it infected the other, and then it became near impossible to stop laughing, and in fact only escalated, overtaxing our shared pair of lungs.

I turned to face O.

"Show me the painting," I said.

O ignored me. Her eyes were glued to my chest. I looked down. The film was playing over and past my breasts, which were too small to disturb the integrity of the image. Only when the film had blacked out in conclusion did O acknowledge me.

"I hope you agree that film suits me much better than painting," she said.

O WAS PACING the room with her arms crossed. She ignored my repeated requests to see the painting. Meanwhile, a black substance was being sprayed onto the bedroom window in periodic bursts, as though by someone handling a garden hose.

"O," I said. "Come on."

"That's not my name anymore."

"What, are you back to Oseol now?"

"No."

"Okay, then what?"

She came to a stop before me.

"I met someone," she said. "I changed my name into a word that only he will ever use. It took me days to decide on the name. I wanted two syllables that had never been conjoined before. I'm sorry if you've been trying to call me. But I had to disconnect my number. I've had to shut off everything so that I can focus on what I'm feeling. Like I'm burning alive. You'll have to keep calling me O, by the way—I just want to make sure you're aware that it's no longer my name even as you keep using it. I need everyone to know they're wrong, so that the feeling of being right can be his alone."

O proceeded to tell her story in a fevered monotone. After dropping me off at Polygon Plaza, she had fallen into a strange mood. She hadn't felt ready to go home. So she got off the subway at Itaewon and walked around until late at night, watching Koreans stumble arm in arm with foreigners down the crowded street. That was when she saw him. He was walking ahead of her, determined to be alone. It moved her to witness his solitude amidst so much anxious socializing. His blue trousers were fraying at the ends, and his black oxfords appeared to be of different sizes. His thick black hair stuck out in all directions with a fresh incorrigibility suggesting that he'd sheared it himself in a moment of crisis. O followed him into a nightclub. She sat at a table in the dark space surrounding the dance floor and watched him enter the fray. Blue lights swung in disorder overhead. The man sporadically bobbed into appearance between other people's heads; it was a curse to see his face so abruptly eclipsed by ones that meant nothing to her. O felt herself swerving into a fatal imbalance at the sight of his beauty. She ordered enough drinks and food to cover her entire table so that she could be disgusted by their comparative mediocrity and leave it all untouched. A menacingly average man stopped by to ask where she could be found online, but she kept her mouth shut, having nothing to tell him, for in that moment, every part of her body was tenaciously unvirtual.

That was how the relationship had begun. Sung was a screenwriter for period dramas, but he had greater ambitions, a desire to sink his probe into the miasmic present. Intrigued by O's story about my love for Moon, he'd suggested they make a short film together.

"We talk so much that we forget to eat sometimes," she said. "Once, we lost track of time entirely and couldn't tell if it was dawn or dusk outside. I felt exquisitely alone with him at that moment, like we were somewhere in the world that no one else could be. Perfectly in between. Benighted together."

I didn't know what to say. The room was getting darker. A tremor was running through the entire building; when I lightly pressed my teeth together, they began to chatter.

"I'm happy for you," I finally said.

"Well, I'm not," O said. "I feel like throwing up all the time. For can there be such a thing as a happy soul? A soul that is fully in the thrum of living?"

O proceeded to say that she regretted having encouraged me to find Moon. She had been lonely and angry; she had wanted to help herself through me. She now suspected that I would persist in my search just to prove a point. But she herself no longer had patience for ideas in their pure form.

"I would love for you to know what this feels like," she said. "I would love for you to feel as badly as I do. But you're headed for a place without answers. So turn back around and dig your heels into a world that's been waiting here for you all along."

"I'm leaving Seoul." The decision had long been made; I was only now awakening to it. "You should come with me."

"No," O said. "I can't do that. The idea of getting on a plane with you and heading in a straight line, but knowing that you're actually making me lost—it scares me."

A thin black film now coated the window in its entirety. The room had grown so dark that I had trouble discerning the expression on O's face. Exhaustion was blooming behind my eyes, and I felt dangerously close to falling asleep. O's voice was all that I could hold on to for orientation. But at the moment she was using it like a knife.

"I wish I were made of glass," I said. "Then you could see right into me. I wouldn't have to say a word to make you understand what I'm feeling."

"It's more likely that I would see right through you," O said. "Which means I wouldn't see you at all. I'd forget you're there and crash into you like a glass wall. Flesh constitutes a tradeoff: it lets you know that a person is standing before you, but you have no idea what this person means."

She came to a crouch before me and peered up at my face.

"O," I said. "Show me the painting."

"You already saw it," she said. "In the film."

"I want to see the real thing."

"You don't know what you're asking for."

O gently pushed aside my legs. Then she reached under the bed, deeper and deeper, until even her head disappeared. She emerged with the painting, her eyes visible just over the canvas. It took me a long time to understand what I was seeing. The back of my left knee was rendered in vivid detail, while the back of my right knee remained a whorl of black strokes.

"One day I'll finish it," she said. "All I need is time."

IN THE LIVING room, we discovered O's mother passed out in front of the veranda. The door was open again. The black substance was everywhere, casting an obsidian shimmer upon the floor, the walls, the furniture. The plasma screen looked the same as before. So did O's mother's black shift. But the chemical speckled every inch of her white skin. The dark sheen upon her body was flawless aside from the area around her mouth, where she seemed to have run a smearing hand.

O fell to her knees and shook her mother by the shoulders. The woman still had her eyes shut as she opened her mouth wide, gasping for words. Her teeth were white, but her tongue was black.

As O cradled her mother's head in her lap, I stepped onto the veranda. Dark fumes obscured my view of the building opposite. The air smelled like it was on fire. I waited for the approach of sirens. But all that could be heard were the shrieks of children playing in the distance.

ABOUT THE AUTHOR

Esther Yi was born in Los Angeles in 1989 and currently lives in Leipzig, Germany.